STRAIGHT
MAN

STRAIGHT MAN

A NOVEL BY

SALLIE BINGHAM

ZOLAND BOOKS

Cambridge, Massachusetts

First edition published in 1996 by
Zoland Books, Inc.
384 Huron Avenue
Cambridge, Massachusetts 02138

PUBLISHER'S NOTE

This book is a work of fiction. Names, characters, places, and
incidents are either the product of the author's imagination
or are used fictitiously. Any resemblance to actual events or
persons, living or dead, is entirely coincidental.

FIRST EDITION

Cover design by Janis Owens
Book design by Boskydell Studio

Printed in the United States of America

02 01 00 99 98 97 96   8 7 6 5 4 3 2 1

This book is printed on acid-free paper, and its binding
materials have been chosen for strength and durability.

Library of Congress Cataloging-in-Publication Data
Bingham, Sallie.
Straight man / Sallie Bingham. — 1st ed.
p.   cm.
ISBN 0-944072-65-8 (alk. paper)
1. Men — Sexual behavior — Fiction. 2. Men —
Psychology — Fiction.
I. Title.
PS3552.I5S77   1996
813'.54 — dc20   96-16398 CIP

STRAIGHT
MAN

1

A HALF INCH of rain in Louisville, a half inch of rain in Cincinnati, an inch in eastern Kentucky: Colby Winn turns down the radio. The headlights' funnel-shaped beams touch the early-morning fog and move it aside, touch the changing trees along the expressway and reach for the black cattle browsing by the shopping center named for a prerevolutionary land grant.

The disc jockey fields a joke, tossed off by the traffic-control pilot, up among the clouds. Traffic comes to a halt, each car caught in its own reflection, flashes of red and yellow light spreading across the wet tarmac.

Rain leaks through the crack in Colby's canvas roof. Rain falls on the knees of his jeans. As he brushes the drops off, the wetness reminds him of the properties and propaganda of a life among strangers — students, associates, women: the last especially. Colby declares to himself that he has never known a dry woman.

There are a good many of the wet ones — liquid, lubricious girls — in the class he is on his way to teach. He is required to teach one class each semester in the graduate school, and he disliked beforehand the types he knew would enroll. The freshmen with their spelling mistakes and intermittent attention are in the right place at the right time, but it is as clear to Colby as it is to the graduate students that they should be somewhere else. The university is about to be cut off at the knees; it will lose its graduate program — there is no more state money for higher education. In a little while, all will be urban studies. Why not Harvard? he wants to ask the five sheep faces staring bleakly up at him in English 501: Hawthorne and Melville. If I went there, you could go there, too. Is it a hopeless love affair with the sycamores and the long fall? — but he never asks, because he wishes to keep what distance he can between himself and their ambitions, their dreadful needs.

He wanted to refuse the assignment, but reason in the form of his great friend I. Weekly's wife prevailed. She reminded him — and she was kneading bread, that was the most powerful reminder: pregnant, and kneading bread — that he had turned down one assignment already (his first semester) in the uses of science in the Victorian novel. I. Weekly's wife, whose name is Martha (by the way, he thinks, attempting to quell the warmth he feels when he thinks of the couple), told him that the department would frown if he turned down another offer.

The department frowning: Colby likes the image. The department is divided into two faces, for him; one large and generally frowning, and another, which contains, for features, Colby and I. Weekly and Martha: two steady eyes and a questing nose. Martha's little beak sniffs up contradictions and blows them out as direct expressions.

She says (from time to time) that Colby's life alone is lack
of freedom, and sometimes Colby agrees. Ten years ago,
when he was married, he was tied hand and foot, and now,
single, he is tied hand and foot. Translating that into its ef-
fects, he feels the horror of the cold place at his feet in his
single bed, of his clothes laid out on the chair the night before, his book on the bed stand where he can find it when he
can't sleep, his electric percolator filed with water and coffee,
to be plugged in as soon as the alarm goes off. His success as
a man alone, he thinks, is really the success of his lack of
freedom, that stone, that brick of a concept, and he switches
the radio to the FM all-rock station and decides to be ado-
lescent for a while.

At the same time, he notices that the gas gauge is on
empty, sees an exit, steps on the accelerator and flies by —
his impulses feel like decorations, feathers in his cap, he
thinks: because it is raining, Monday morning, early October, and if he runs out of gas, something new is sure to happen.

He switches in this way from time to time, mostly late
at night when he drinks Scotch or smokes some pot until
he can go to sleep. Then he sometimes sees the fortunate
chosen form of his life: the freshman faces, little Andrea
Wesker in his graduate classes, the Weeklys, who feed and
warm him, and he knows that lack of freedom is just another name for happiness, as a song says. He likes to hear
what the songs say when it is raining a half inch in
Louisville, a half inch in Cincinnati and an inch in eastern
Kentucky.

Taking his exit, leaning hard to the left, Colby sees a

woman standing by the side of the turnoff. She is wearing jeans, no coat, her left thumb is out, and in her right hand she is holding a Coke bottle. Colby sees her cap of hair, darkened by the rain, and thinks she must be hitching from one forbidden place to another. Then he notices that the top is on the Coke bottle and thinks she must be looking for somebody who has an opener and he has one, on a leather thong tied to his belt: a Swiss army knife his father gave him. It has ten blades, a toothpick, a pair of tweezers, scissors, a corkscrew and a bottle opener.

He is beyond her. He stops the car.

In the rearview mirror, he sees her loping towards him. She grabs the doorhandle and shakes it until he leans across and flips up the lock. She opens the door and jumps in.

He sees the damp knees of her jeans and the edge of her pulled-looking white sweater and then she says, "Hey, thanks!"

"Where to?" he asks.

"Downtown."

"I'm going to Third Street."

"Can I get something to eat?"

"Sure." A truck passes, swatting his windshield with spray, and Colby turns on the wipers and then looks at her. Sharp nose and a small mouth, open. She is pale in the headlight glare.

"You passing through?" he asks.

"Stopping for a while — if I can get work."

"From where to where?"

"I started in Cincinnati."

"You didn't get far," he says, passing the truck; the steering wheel vibrates and he slows down.

"Far enough." She puts a blunt hand on each knee and Colby wonders where she learned her gruff talk. She hits a high mountain whine, but most of her words are pronounced in neutral.

"Where are you trying to get to, eventually?" he asks.

"I told you I want to eat."

"OK." He smells the wet wool of her sweater and is surprised it's not Orlon. It looks like a sweater knitted by a loving but untalented relative. One arm is a good deal wider than the other, and her hand, at the end of it, looks wired on. She is carrying a worn knapsack. He glances at her large feet, planted side by side on his floorboard, snatches the car out of a wide curve and is surprised by her well-made, well-used leather hiking boots.

Then he sees thin legs, boylike, sharp knees inside the jeans. The jeans are old, worn, not very clean — he imagines she sleeps in them. As she turns her head, catching his glance, her dark hair flips against her pale cheek, and he notices the contrast: strange, enticing. Her eyes are shadowed, some kind of green.

"Watch out," she says.

Traffic is thickening as they approach town, and he leans forward into the windshield, both hands clutching the wheel.

"Here it is." He waves. "There used to be a sign here, red and green lights, Gateway to the South, it said, but they did away with it."

"Why is everything torn down?"

"You know how it is — boom times, federal money, big dreams on the part of the happy few, and the next thing you know, the whole town has been torn down." Then he feels obliged to ask, "Where are you going after this?"

"Down the Ohio to the Mississippi and then down the Mississippi to the Gulf."

"On a raft?"

She doesn't get it. "I'm counting on hitching."

"How will you live?"

"I'll stop along the way at the reggies. Regional theaters," she translates. "If all else fails, I'll get a job onboard the boat that takes medicines down to Guatemala. I've done that before. I'm an actress," she adds, unnecessarily. "He takes medicines down for the missionaries and brings their handmade jewelry back."

"An actress!" he exclaims, then adds, quickly, "How long is all this going to take?"

"I have two months. Mama goes in the hospital the Monday after Thanksgiving. I have till then."

"What made you want to go down the rivers?"

"I've lived in the mountains all my life. I never have seen much running water, except for creeks." She pronounces it "cricks."

"I thought you said you started from Cincinnati. Plenty of water in Cincinnati!"

"I said that," she agrees.

She does not add anything.

"You want the top off that Coke bottle?" he asks, after a while.

"Just don't do it with your teeth."

He laughs, tweaks the leather thong, and the knife flips

out on the seat. She reaches across for it. He feels a light tug on the thong. "Don't cut yourself."

"I knew somebody once had one of these. It wasn't anywhere near as thick but the opener was in the same place." She is prying up the opener with her thumbnail, and Colby sees that her nails are all short and tough enough to be used.

She hooks the opener under the cap and again he feels a light tug on the thong.

The cap shoots off and soda bubbles over her hand and she wipes it on the seat.

"Here," he says, nudging his box of tissues towards her, but she is already drinking. He cannot look again because they are at Spaghetti Junction, where all the main routes for the Midwest intersect.

Later he is able to look. She is tipping her head back, and he sees the wave motion of swallows in her throat. She must be terribly thirsty. She must also be terribly thin to have so little meat on her throat. He remembers watching chickens dip their beaks in water and then tip their heads up to let it roll back — giving thanks.

She sighs, wiping her mouth on the back of her hand, and Colby swerves to avoid a Chevrolet that is taking the exit for St. Louis.

"Give me some," he says. The tone of his voice is novel. "Please," he adds. She hands him the bottle.

The Coke is bubbly and warm. He gets nothing but the fizz. He hands the bottle back. "You must have been carrying this for a while."

"Couple of hours. Guy at the gas station started to get fresh and I left without opening it."

Colby shakes his head fiercely. "That kind of thing makes me sick!"

"Does it?"

"Ought to have more respect," he grumbles.

"Yes," she says, seriously.

"Ought to be taught more respect!"

"I agree with you. Are you going to do it?"

"You may just be surprised." Saying it, he realizes how much he wants to please her.

"I guarantee I'll give you an opportunity," she says impulsively.

He wonders if she is flirting. "Let's get some breakfast." They are weaving under the legs of the bridge, the river on their right, sunk between its banks behind a pair of partially dismantled cranes and a heap of driftwood from last spring's flood.

"It looks just like Cincinnati," she says. "They treat the river like a sewer."

"Well, we're trying," Colby says. "We've got a committee fighting pollution."

Starting up Third Street, Colby begins to worry about getting to his class. "All these towns are more or less the same. Big and poor and ugly," he says vaguely. Then he decides that if he is efficient, he will be able to treat her to breakfast and get to his class only a few minutes late. "I want to take you to someplace nice," he says briskly; they are passing the topless shoeshine parlor. "I don't have much time."

"You on your way to work?"

"I teach at the university. What's your name?" he asks, realizing they are going to separate soon. He needs something to hang on to.

She looks at him. "I don't know your name, Mister."

"I'm sorry. I should have introduced myself. Colby Winn."

He lets go of the steering wheel and reaches out his hand. She touches his palm with the tips of five cool fingers. "Ann Lee Crabtree."

"Ann Lee?" He tests the name. "How old are you?"

"Twenty-nine."

"You look about fifteen."

"Not if you see my hands."

He glances and nearly runs off the road.

"Grubbing up 'seng. We sell it, at home," she explains.

"You mean that root?"

"Ginseng. I don't make any special claims for it. They like it in China, those places."

"You grub it up with your hands?"

"It breaks if you use something. That's a forked root — it's tender. My grandmother used to say if you break it, it screams like a baby."

Colby remembers Shakespeare's mandrake root. Behind that, he remembers stories he heard in Pineville and the way his father laughed. Ginseng is an aphrodisiac, the Orientals claim.

He swings into TIMMYS, where in a wild moment he recently took Andrea Wesker for a plate of ribs. "They'll feed us well here," he promises as he shoots the car into a slot, and then, for the first time in months, he feels his stomach churn as though remembering appetite.

"Breakfast?" She's examining the place.

"It's a night place, they have a bar and a jukebox. It's a breakfast place, too — see the sign?"

She looks at it. There are gold fleur-de-lis around the edges. "I don't have much money."

"I'll treat." He has not thought of this before, but now it seems obvious: he wants to treat her like the lady she probably isn't. He swings out of the car before she can answer, hurries around to her side and opens the door, holding out his hand to help her out of the low seat.

She avoids his hand, slips out under his arm and smiles.

Then she waits for him to open the restaurant door, and Colby thinks she is preparing herself for the assault of strangers' eyes. In fact there is nothing to prepare. The short hair on the back of her head is still as smooth as the side of a cup and the white sweater is pulled down to her hips and she has no coat to slip off.

"Women are funny about coats," he says, adding quickly, "You don't even have one."

"You mean being helped with them?"

"I knew a girl once" — knew, he thinks, is an odd choice of verb — "who used to let her coat drop on the floor just for the pleasure of seeing me pick it up. How come you started out on your travels with no coat?" He opens the door and shoos her in.

She stops in the foyer: plastic trays full of dirty dishes, a lighted glass candy case without much in it and a jukebox playing "Late Date."

"If I need a coat, I'll beg, borrow or steal one," she says.

"You don't mean steal."

She doesn't answer. A work-worn waitress comes to show them to a table. It has not been cleared, and Ann Lee lifts her elbows out of the way while the waitress scoops dishes and glasses into a plastic bin. Ann Lee holds her elbows up in the air while the waitress wipes the table with a rusty-looking sponge. Then Ann Lee places her elbows on either side of a fresh paper mat, decorated with pictures of the state shrines.

"You live with your family?" Colby asks, reaching for a tall menu and passing it to her.

She accepts the menu but continues to look at the shrines. "I've been to Natural Bridge. It wasn't much. My little brother cried. He thought it was going to fall."

"What? The bridge?"

"Jimmy was seven — the youngest."

"How many of you are there?"

"Four," she says, adding generously, "I'm the oldest girl. A brother ahead of me, Derrick, gone to De-troit." She makes it two words in the mountain way. "Then Caroline and Jimmy."

"You might want to order." He is eager to enjoy his own appetite before it departs.

She is still looking at the mat. "I think I've seen that statue of Daniel Boone. Doesn't it stand up high somewhere?"

"Frankfort?" he asks, although he knows. "I'm new here, myself, I haven't been to any of those places" — and remembers his mother, in Pineville, saying on Sunday afternoons, "Let's go somewhere, let's get in the car and go."

He tries to hook her attention away from the shrines. "I just moved down here from New York. Came down for the start of the term. Out of the blue. Twenty years teaching in Cambridge and New York and then, a poet and teacher named Isaiah Weekly offered me a job. Just like that. I thought, Why not?"

"I go where they give me work, too."

He decides not to discuss his sudden decision. She can have no idea of the pain. "You work in Cincinnati?"

"What about the Breaks of Sandy? You been there?" She is still studying the mat.

"I told you I'm new here. The furthest I've been yet is to the library in Indiana. The library here is inferior."

"Bad-mouthing," she says. "Louisville! That was the big city, to us. It makes me remember those books about girls and horses and the girls getting their way. I liked those."

"The Little Colonel. That girl was spoiled. Anyway, it was supposed to take place in Lexington, wasn't it?"

"I didn't know boys read that book. It happened right here in Louisville."

"Did you have a bookmobile, or what?"

"What about Pineville? You ever been to Pineville? Site of the first Civil War battle fought on Kentucky soil?"

"First and last. I told you, I came down here in August" — he says and wonders about the nature of his lies.

"From New York?"

"Yes. I was teaching there, at Columbia, after I left Cambridge."

'Sounds like you've lived in a lot of places," she says, without much interest, but she is looking at him, and Colby sees that her eyes are light gray, tin-colored, with fine blond lashes. "Are you married?"

"Divorced. Almost ten years." The way he says it shames him for the first time. This explanation has been the usual badge, hardly in need of elaboration.

Ann Lee is staring. "Divorced?"

"It took a while."

"And now she's stranded."

"Hardly. She's got a boyfriend."

"A married woman?"

"We're divorced."

"You give her money?"

"That's the law of the land."

"What about your kids? Don't you worry about your kids?"

"We didn't have any children," he says, and this explanation, too, which has always been so easy — no time, no hope, no desire — is as heavy as the admission of a major sin.

"You were married how long? I want to eat," she adds, catching sight of the menu in her hand. She spreads it on the table.

"Nearly eleven years."

"I want waffles, if you're paying —" He repeats that he is. "Not that I all the time let the man pay, but you look like you can afford it. What do you make, teaching?"

"Enough."

She unfolds her paper napkin and sinks it into her lap, pressing out bubbles of air. Now Colby would like to talk about his marriage, but it is too late: she is only thinking about food. "Is that lady going to take our order?" she asks.

He beckons to the waitress. "What makes you think I can afford the waffles?" he asks Ann Lee.

"Your clothes. Your car."

"This old jacket?" He is wearing a worn herringbone tweed.

"It cost something in the beginning," she says.

"You all want to eat?" the waitress asks.

"Waffles for the lady," Colby says. "Bacon? Sausage? Pure Vermont syrup — synthetic all the way to the bottom of the bottle?" Ann Lee ducks her head each time. "All of that," he tells the waitress. "Just coffee for me."

"You already ate?" Ann Lee asks.

"I lost my appetite," he says, looking around at the big room, the shipwrecked tables and chairs. Rain is drumming on a tin roof somewhere, a dismal country sound. He begins to worry again about his class and jumps to his feet. "I have to telephone."

Colby flies to the pay phone in the hall and drops in a dime. His fingers are weak, dialing, and he makes a mistake and has to start over again. I. Weekly answers, sounding rushed.

"Listen, I. I'm stuck. Can you take over for me?"

"Stuck? Where?"

"Just stuck. I'm going to be late for my class."

I. sighs, a long windy sound down the wire. "All right. You never asked before."

"I'll be down there in a while." Colby hangs up, but even his thirst is quenched now and he wonders why he is hurrying back to the table. He has never asked anyone to cover for him before, it is unthinkable — he is betraying everything he believes in. He cannot understand why he is sliding into his seat, stirring sugar into his coffee.

"What happened?" Ann Lee asks.

"Well, my class. I'm going to be late."

"Go on. Get started."

"I don't want to go on. I want to sit here with you —" he says and realizes that, for a little while, that is so. He wants to stay with her as usually he only wants sleep, or food; something obvious, essential.

"Sit here with me with those kids waiting?"

"They're not kids, they're graduate students. Don't worry, I have a friend covering for me."

"When they expect you? You go, or I will."

He sees her beginning to unfold from beneath the table and, at the same time, he sees the waitress coming with her waffles. He knows that she will eat but he will not — he probably will not even drink his coffee. "All right," he says and starts to get up. Suddenly he feels warm, really warm for the first time in weeks; he is starting to sweat. "All right," he repeats. He begins to go through his pockets for four or five dollars to leave for her meal; Ann Lee watches while he decides on a five and presses it out flat on the table. "Where will you be?" he asks. "When am I going to —"

"I'll be at the theater, if they give me a job." She takes the five-dollar bill and folds it into a square packet and stores it up the tighter sleeve of her sweater. "If they have a part for me, I'll stay here awhile."

He wants to ask her if she has a resumé, pictures, all that, but is afraid of insulting her. "All right!" he exclaims and starts for the door.

As he walks, his warmth begins to fade and he dreads the cold outside, the dash to his car, the rain. He dreads going to his class, dreads interrupting I., who will be sitting on the edge of Colby's desk with one leg in its wrinkled pipestem jean swinging slowly back and forth. Colby will never get the students on track after I. slides out the door. It will probably turn out that I. has been reading them poetry.

Eight forty-five.

A digital watch, he thinks, as he looks at his old-fashioned one; that's what I need. These hands are too hard to read. He hurries to his car. His hair is wet again. Inside, he smells Ann Lee's soapy child smell and begins to imagine the drive to the theater, down Broadway, right on Fourth — no, a right turn's not allowed there — right on Fifth, or is it one way the other way? — and then around to Liberty, Jefferson, Main. It will take him nine minutes, he figures, from the university, door to door.

2

DURING CLASS, Colby is distracted. The students annoy
him in the midst of his distraction and he wants to shout at
them to get out, quit listening, quit looking, even. His calf
muscles jump with the impulse to get out himself if they
won't. He is talking garbage, and the garbage is made from
the pure gold of the books he loves.

While the class dithers, Colby remembers a label from the
first year after his divorce when his ideas were floating
around, broken loose, broken up, no longer part of any particular whole. He was in therapy then, and the doctor used
the label to goad him: Instant Gratification, I.G., he called
it. The first time Colby heard that, he sat up straight in his
chair because he had never expected such a title. It seemed a
kind of honor. Then the therapist repeated it too often and
Colby used the nickname to protect himself. Whenever he
ate a fat snack or stayed up too late or smoked too much pot,
Colby would look at himself curiously, doing this unlikely
thing, and repeat what the sandy-haired fox of a therapist
had called him: Instant Grat.

At last class is over. It is nearly ten; Colby goes to the

library and sits for a while, fingering his discontent. He knows better than to continue alone in the midst of such turbulent currents. He starts for the cafeteria and finds I. in line with his tray.

"I was wondering if I could drop in this evening," Colby says, taking the next place in line.

"I'll have to ask Martha," I. says, helping himself to mashed sweet potatoes, a plateful.

Colby stares.

"She's ready to have the baby any day now, Col. She might not feel up to company."

"Company!"

"Her back's been bothering her a lot."

"When will you know?"

I. finally sees his expression and says, "Right now." He puts the plate of sweet potatoes down on the nearest table and Colby deposits his bratwurst and sauerkraut and they turn together to the cafeteria door. They march through it to a pay phone. I. needs a dime; Colby shuffles it out of his pocket and cleans off a bit of lint.

The dime trickles through the mechanism and Colby, waiting to hear the dial tone, thinks that the noises of telephones have been the music of his life. He remembers waiting in phone booths in Cambridge for his ex-wife, then his fiancée, to return his call; Colby never had any money in those days, not even a nickel for overtime, although sometimes, unbeknownst to Laura, he had an unchanged five-dollar bill buried in his pocket. His mother occasionally sent five-dollar bills through the mail, squeezing them out of her grocery money; Colby never spent any of them. Money has never been forthcoming, and Colby is not ashamed of that.

The line is busy and I. hangs up and they wait in silence. Permission has never been needed before. Colby distracts himself by thinking of other telephones, of the faint digestive hums and clicks while he waited for Laura to call back; she was usually in the midst of studying and loath to lose more than three minutes. In his dormitory room, he sometimes imagined hearing calls from her coming down the wire; there would be a faint anticipatory hum or startle in the telephone at his elbow.

Later, when they were married, Colby lost the knack of hoping for her calls. Even when he was installed in the office on the floor under his father-in-law, he would hear the telephone ring upstairs without forewarning. Often the call concerned him. Laura never exactly complained but she kept her father informed. Now and then Professor McKee telephoned Colby to pass along the information — "I hear you've been a little depressed lately" — but even then, Colby did not foresee the call. After his divorce, his ex-father-in-law never called him directly; instead he sent what Colby thought of as vicious rays down to Columbia to scorch his career.

I. is dialing again, and now he says, "Honey?" Colby is surprised. He does not think "Honey" is in I.'s vocabulary.

"She says what about tomorrow," I. reports, a minute later. He looks at the floor near Colby's feet. "It seems she's tired. Could you come after supper?"

"Certainly," Colby says. "I have a lot of work to do tonight, papers . . ." How fast his disappointment subsides, turning into a sour kind of satisfaction.

I. talks a little longer to his wife and then hangs up. Colby dogs him back into the cafeteria, where their plates have cooled. They sit down opposite each other, alone at a long table in the middle of the crowd; I. takes a spoonful of sweet potato and asks, "What's wrong?"

"I can't get started on that paper I have to give in Chicago."

"You'll like Chicago," I. says.

"Ideas of death in *Middlemarch*. It's too small."

"Sounds too big to me," I. says. "Got an outline?" He is shoveling sweet potatoes, and Colby sees their orange color reflected in I.'s glasses. He is very thin and tall, with a bird-like fragility which makes Colby feel stocky.

"Those potatoes agree with your looks," Colby says.

"Where are you stuck?"

"I haven't written a word."

"Well, it's six months off. Just sit down and get started. Just sit down. Why do I have to tell you that?"

"Why are you a vegetarian?"

"It's not so much principle as instinct. Two years ago when Martha miscarried I lost my taste for meat."

"I'm not sure I want to see the connection," Colby says, but it is too late. He puts down his bratwurst. "Something happens when you get close to forty, you don't seem to need to eat in the middle of the day."

"Speak for yourself," I. says, munching a cracker.

"Where does all that food go?"

I. laughs. His small blues eyes bulge. "I get rid of it. I get rid of a lot of baggage, somehow."

"Like your name. You cut that down to size. Not to go through life burdened with the Old Testament." Then he wants to get the conversation back on track before I. starts on another account of his coon-hunting mother and her misused gift for choosing names. "I'm bone lonely, that's the trouble," Colby says.

I. does not even stop chewing.

"I used to be used to it, but I don't want to be used to it anymore." He is forming the conviction as he speaks. "Most of the time, there's enough noise in my head, preoccupations, so I don't notice the quiet outside. But if I broke my leg, nobody'd come."

"I'd come. When you planning on breaking it?" Colby's smile is dim and I. pulls himself together. "You ought to try talking to your students."

"They are meant to talk to me."

"What about Andrea Wesker? I thought you were going to get to know her. That might cure the ache in your bones."

"Hands off undergraduates but graduate students are fair game. I don't allow anyone to dictate to me in that department."

"Who's trying to dictate?"

"You know that memo. I plan to stay away from all of them, boycott the deal."

"Then don't complain to me about lonely. Half those girls would jump on you — "

"I had it with girls in New York. I told you about Mimi. I didn't have an inch of life left to call my own. Running out late at night to take care of her friends. 'He's got a crisis, he must be a Pisces.' Trying to clear a space in her belongings to put down my papers. Trying to get her friends out of the apartment so I could have some peace; they were all the time 'crashing,' filling the air with their fumes. . . . Then she'd come jumping on me like a wild thing, middle of the night."

"I thought you liked that little Andrea Wesker," I. says indulgently.

"Like her! I took her out for ribs once and she's been calling me Dr. Winn ever since."

"The others call you what?"

"I told them to use my first name as soon as they thought they knew me well enough. Everybody but the Indian was calling me Col by the end of the first week."

"What does the Indian call you?"

"Nothing."

"The rest of them know you?" I. asks, then hurries ahead. "You ought to spend more time with us."

This is the opportunity Colby has been waiting for. He seizes it grimly. "After the baby is born, you two aren't going to have much time."

"You can help out."

"How?"

"You can rock him."

"What if it's a girl?"

"I'll let you rock her till she's eighteen. Come on, Col, cheer up. Martha was saying the other day she still wishes you'd taken the apartment across the street."

"Too close for comfort. Wear out my welcome even faster. Besides, I like where I am."

"That fern farm. Well, it's beautiful. But you live on your plants instead of on your furniture."

"I love them," Colby says haughtily. "They don't ask for a damn thing, except water."

"They don't even want sun, being ferns." I. sighs. "How you can stand living that close to the stockyards."

"I only smell it when the wind is from the south. I like that lowing."

"On their way to be slaughtered!"

"Yeah, but I'm part of a resurrecting neighborhood. We're going to have a competition for the best flower box, next spring. There isn't anywhere else you can get a shotgun house for eighteen thousand dollars," he reminds I., who, of all things, likes money.

"And bone lonely," I. says. "You've just got to come see us more often. Six o'clock OK?" I. stands up.

"I told you I'd come after dinner."

"You ever plan to eat?" I. drops his hand on Colby's shoulder. The hand lies there like a leaf. Colby would love I. to stay with him; the only way to make that happen would be to launch into a description of Ann Lee amusing enough to keep I.'s attention but false enough to leave her unharmed. So he tells about the Coke bottle and the hiking boots and the job at the theater.

When he has finished, I. bends down and looks Colby in the face. "This is the reason, isn't it?"

"No. That's not what I mean. It was a kind of an entertainment."

I. closes his hand on Colby's shoulder and says, "Come to dinner. Martha is going to fix bean soup. Just come — it won't matter." And then he is off, loping, long-legged and thin as a crane, his green sweater-vest loose over his hips, his wrinkled blue jeans riding up.

Colby wonders why I. puts up with him. Loneliness

draws him, Colby thinks; I. knew something about that before he married — and the things that may sprout from
loneliness, unexpected, even shocking. Colby doesn't mind
adding a little spice to his friends' mild lives. He knows he
would do almost anything to keep them wanting him: the
one warm spot in a cold world.

3

IT IS THE NEXT DAY, and Colby hasn't tried to see Ann Lee — he is proud of that — twenty-four hours, a whole day — when he gets into his car and starts to the theater. The theater and the zoo are his two favorite places; he found them both within a week after he arrived. They are housed in old buildings turned to new uses, the zoo in the gardener's cottage, walled garden, stable and greenhouse of one of the big old river places; the theater is what Colby remembers to have been a very satisfactory ten-cent store.

He parks near Fourth Street, which has been turned into a mall, and walks down an expanse of cement lined with large empty planters. The mall has hit a snag; it is more attractive to blacks, whose neighborhood it borders, than to whites, who can no longer cruise in the safety of their cars but must meet these creations of their lurid imagination (and Colby is passing one now, in pink knee breeches and a blond wig). So the specialty shops have been replaced by wiggeries and record palaces. Some are empty, their display windows like abandoned rooms, littered with newspaper.

He passes a record store blaring rock music; the electric instruments in a window gleam. Next door, the cafeteria where once as a child Colby ate Saturday lunch with his father because of the collard greens is still open, although the waitresses, lined up inside the long window, look like apathetic soldiers manning a low barricade.

The gold letters on the big red sign spell out TEN-CENT THEATER. Colby has heard this called a joke since the theater tickets here are actually twice as expensive as they are in Cincinnati, where the theater is called THE ROYAL BOX.

He stops to look at the display windows, which are as large as he remembers, big enough for a harvest of gadgets — the miracle potato peeler, the carpet sweeper that works without hands. He remembers watching the carpet sweeper displayed, inside the store, by a very small woman who worked it entirely with her feet. Colby expected that she would have no hands, but in fact her hands were noticeable, tipped with scarlet polish, the first polish Colby had ever seen.

That time, Colby was supposed to look for a birthday present for his mother. He studied jars of pink bath salts, fish-shaped bottles of lotion for detergent hands, rubbery bubbles of bath oil. Meanwhile, his father silently hurried him. Colby dawdled until his father said, "Come on, get it over with, we don't have all day." He had urgent business at the hardware store. Finally Colby chose a fish-shaped bottle.

Now the long windows are sparsely arrayed with pots made by a local group. The pots seem low in such great height; they crouch on yellow crepe paper. A large mass of flowers at the center seems to be made out of pipestem cleaners and crepe paper, like the flowers Colby's mother made for his birthdays. Colby is leaning closer to examine the flowers when a man's voice, at his elbow, requests him kindly to move along, and he looks down at Mr. Marvin Toast, coming with his broom and dustpan.

"Morning, Mr. Toast," Colby says with the smile he has seen on other people's faces. Colby knows him from the newspaper.

Mr. Toast does not answer; he is busy with his broom. Colby gets out of the way at the last minute and Mr. Toast whisks by. "It's the litter keeps the right people away," he remarks.

"You certainly are right about that," Colby says. It is hard to decide whether Mr. Toast is crazy, so he is treated with fence-sitting condescension; Colby is ashamed to find himself adopting the same attitude. It may turn out that Mr. Toast is the town's most devoted philanthropist (which will only be revealed in his will), or he may be finally, sorrowfully committed. Mr. Toast is seventy-five; he used to own the biggest department store in town (now moved to the suburbs), so his late personal eccentricity is bewildering. After he retired, he sold his big house and moved to a one-room apartment in town; as far as anyone knows, all he keeps there are his clothes and his broom.

At this point, Colby feels his own condescension like a thorn and hurries through the double doors.

Inside, long red velvet curtains divide the large space into a lobby, box office, business office and several rehearsal areas. The main stage is approached through tunnels of apricot-colored satin. Colby waits until he hears noises which tell him what is happening in each of the curtained alcoves; once, in a wandering fit, he passed through a space where a naked woman was being soberly fitted to a hat. Now he hears the apprentices sawing in the cellar and, when they stop, a voice reading; he starts towards it.

He pushes the curtain aside and only wonders at his courage when he sees Grant Tom, the director, who is standing on a small platform facing Ann Lee.

"Yes?" Grant Tom says.

"I'm a friend of hers," Colby says and waits for Ann Lee to turn around and recognize him. She does not.

Grant Tom stares as though trying to remember the name, and Colby realizes that in this town, anyone in a tweed jacket may be a member of the board.

"We're rehearsing," Grant Tom says, at last.

"I know. I'd like to observe, if I may," Colby says grandly and takes a folding chair.

"Why, yes," Grant Tom says. "Sit down. We'll take a five-minute break."

Finally Ann Lee turns, and Colby sees that she is enjoying herself. "It's all right, Grant," she says as she drifts towards Colby.

"Five minutes," Grant Tom repeats warningly.

"I don't want five minutes," Ann Lee says, arrested in her flow. "Just let's go on with the reading and let him stay. For his education," she adds, flirtatiously.

Grant Tom hesitates. Colby sees that he is faced with deciding, this early on, how much Ann Lee counts. "All right," he says finally, and Colby knows that Ann Lee's career at the Ten-Cent is made.

Yet she is still dressing the part of a hitchhiker, her hairy-fringed jeans not even very clean, her T-shirt so loose it does not show her breasts, a dismal cardigan over her shoulders.

"All my life in a shithouse," a voice cues, and Colby turns to see the eternal helper, a pale blond, sitting on a chair in the corner.

Ann Lee lifts her chin a fraction, and Colby willingly sees her transformed: her thin shoulders fan out until her long narrow body seems suspended from its own wings. Yet the words she speaks are commonplace. It is the way she places the words, midway in a space of air, which affects him; she has a dangling grace. "No more men." Colby can see the dubious question mark she hangs on the end of the sentence.

"A little less tenuous," Grant Tom says. "Remember, you are making comparisons. You have that kind of mind. Categorizing. 'Last year, that man. This year, this man. And what difference does it make?'"

"I'm glad I also get to do Chekhov," Ann Lee says with a sigh. 'Last year, that man. This year, this man. And what difference does it make?'"

"But compare. Let us hear the comparison. Just the tone," he says.

She tries it again, with greater clarity. The question mark now is inked in. Colby would like to protest but knows his place.

Now she begins to speak about love, its disappointments, and Colby sees that it is hard for her to control her enthusiasm. She takes a step backwards as though to throw her winged body into shadow but the result is to set her off even more dramatically against the red curtain. "Now I want to live my own life in my own way," she chants and goes on in this vein until Grant Tom holds up his hand.

"You are going to have to listen to me," he says. "This girl is not a lady."

"Why, Mr. Tom, I'm hardly a lady myself."

"Well, you're making her into one. You had the right tone earlier, kind of sulky" — and he casts a glance at Colby as though his presence is to blame. "Throw the lines out," he tells Ann Lee. "Don't be quite so careful." He stands up and with his right hand rearranges her shoulder blades, drooping her wings.

Colby is horrified to see him touching her. "You're *poor*," Grant Tom is saying. "Poor and weak and frail."

"But I must have learned something in jail," Ann Lee insists. "I see me proud."

"Proud, with an illegitimate baby, a prison record and no future?"

"Does anybody ever think that way?"

Grant Tom sighs. "I guess you still haven't learned. You walked in here just like the first time with your own kind of ideas. I guess you don't want to hear about other points of view, other ways of doing things. I guess you would like to do this your own way."

Colby is frightened, realizing that his presence has ignited this tirade. He does not know where Grant Tom will stop. He wonders if Ann Lee is working for the minimum and if this fact will bring Grant Tom up short. Then he realizes that the director has veered off into a more or less harmless though intense history of his theater, how it was a nothing, a dinner playhouse with food so bad the patrons paid to miss

the meal and such poor productions patrons had to praise
the scenery and even the lights; how he has brought it up
from nowhere with seven years of hard work, raising money
as well as directing; how now at last the thing is done and he
has his audience in the palm of his hand, and is not about
to give away the pleasure, the pride and the accomplish-
ment . . . He doesn't get any further because he catches Ann
Lee's eye.

"If you don't want me . . ." She drops her script on the
floor.

"Now don't go jumping to conclusions."

Colby gets up, goes over and picks up the script. He
hands it to her, but her hand is so relaxed the script drops
again. He picks it up and puts it on the table.

"I am not used to this treatment," Ann Lee says, looking
around as though for a coat.

"I mean, consider your options." Grant Tom gets up hur-
riedly. "We're a family here, we take care of our people."

"I don't want to be taken care of. There's River Region
Theater, down at Cairo," she adds.

"Minerva Potts still messing around down there. No vision, no money, they only pay expenses. Besides, right now
they're doing a black Hamlet."

"Then I'll go further south."

"Look, I like you, you know that," Grant Tom says, holding out his hand. "You could fit in here the way you did before. I'm sure of it." When she does not trouble to reply, he
turns to Colby. "Your friend here will certainly agree . . ."

Colby does not hear the rest because he is struck by what
he sees in Grant Tom's face: the hope, the need which Colby

never expected or wanted to see in that granular, well-closed countenance. Now "your friend here." Colby realizes that his weight is required in the balance; he is solid, although Ann Lee still does not appear to recognize him. He wonders if Grant Tom will recognize him the next time they meet and imagines the ill-concealed embarrassment with which the director will mention that situation.

She must be working for the minimum.

Grant Tom may also have personal reasons for wanting to keep her in town.

"Tell me about the play," Colby orders.

Grant Tom, distracted, mutters, "It's just a work in progress, social realism, life in the prison system and out. Written by one of our local people."

"Violence?"

"Oh no, that's all in her past, we'll handle it with one flashback."

"Sex?"

"What do you think? This is a play about loneliness."

"Then I think it would have sex in it," Colby says.

"It's a good part," Ann Lee announces, and while the two men watch, she goes over to the table and picks up the script. The air is lifted by an anonymous sigh of relief.

"It certainly ought to be," Colby says, adding hastily, "What about a contract?" He knows he is stepping into un-familiar water.

"You don't appear to be familiar with the situation," Grant Tom says. "This is not New York."

"She has to have some kind of security. How long is the run?"

"We don't even have understudies, can't afford them."

"I thought you said in the palm of your hand!"

"That's purely psychological."

"What do you pay here?"

Ann Lee sighs loudly and turns back.

"Union scale," Grant Tom says wearily. "What is your connection, exactly?"

"I'm her friend." Embarrassed, Colby adds, "She's new here, she could maybe use some advice."

"She's not new here," Grant Tom says, man to man.

Ann Lee speaks to Colby. "Look, I've decided. I'm staying here. There are worse situations. You can stop now — Colby," she adds.

He is so astonished that she remembers his name (although his restless, unwearying suspicions are not quieted and he realizes he does not expect her to remember his last name) that he does not hear much of the rest of the reading. Grant Tom has made up his mind; Ann Lee has made up her mind; nothing else really matters.

Later, Grant Tom tells her, "You can take a room at the Mayflower, we have a special arrangement. It's a pretty good deal. You can walk back and forth. Where are your things?"

"I'll buy what I need."

He hisses with admiration.

"I travel light," she says, and Colby sees that she is basking. He is treated to a brilliant vision of Ann Lee lying between the director's legs. It is his first sexual flash in a long time, and he interprets the jerk of his penis as pain.

"Let's get out of here," he says, taking her arm, meaning simply to escort her, but his fingers close down hard and she protests: "You're hurting me, Colby!" Surprised, he relaxes his grip.

"See you, kids," Grant Tom says, smiling.

Colby propels her through the velvet tunnel out onto the sidewalk and then cannot remember whether or not it is time for a meal. He looks at the mall clock, a giant daisy whose petals close and open at noon. People are gathered to watch this event, so he knows it is nearly time for lunch.

"What about something to eat? We could go to the cafeteria," he says, adding, "Or are you a vegetarian?"

"I don't think enough about it to be," she says. "All right." She is neither eager nor bored. She gives him custody of her arm again, and he is surprised by the rapid healing of her trust.

She says, "You certainly tried to help me, in there!"

"Did I?"

She doesn't answer, giving him a dimpling smile that alerts his suspicions. "What did you do all day yesterday?" he asks.

"Oh, I walked around town, made an appointment at the theater."

"Where did you spend the night?"

"At a motel," she says breezily.

"A motel."

"I rode the bus to get there." She knows him well enough already to interpret his tone, and she smiles, smugly.

He does not believe her, does not believe anything, suddenly, and he says sadly, "I guess I was a darned fool for trying to help."

She does not say anything.

Colby steers her to the cafeteria, still pressing her arm a little too hard; he feels the bone. He expects it to feel porous as coral but instead realizes he is gripping something solid. He realizes at the same time that he is getting an erection.

"Let's get something hot to eat," he says avidly.

She allows him to guide her through the door into the Rainbow Cafeteria. As the door closes behind them, Colby hears the first canned notes of the noon carillon and knows the daisy clock is folding its petals.

Ann Lee stops to look at the steamboat pictures hung high on the walls, and Colby notices as though it is his fault that the walls are the stale blue color he remembers from childhood. The balcony with its toy train display has been shut down until further notice: "That used to kind of fascinate me," he tells Ann Lee, "that little German train chugging along through paper mountains and trees, all year long, with little lights strung up at Christmas."

"I'm hungry," Ann Lee says.

"We have to get trays and go up to the counter, first. My father used to love the collard greens."

At the nearest table, Marvin Toast, his broom propped beside him, is dunking doughnuts into a cup of coffee. He dunks the doughnuts whole, one at a time, then sets them out on his plate to drain. "Best coffee in town. If they knew, they'd come here, those East End ladies eating yogurt with their maids."

Ann Lee stops to listen.

Mr. Toast looks at her with appreciation, and Colby imagines that the old man is noticing the ends of her hair, curling like the feathers on a drake's tail.

"I am the conscience of this town," Mr. Toast explains.

"I believe you," Ann Lee says. "I'm opening in a play here in two weeks, and I want you to tell everybody you see to come."

"What's it called?"

"*Going All the Way,* but that doesn't mean anything. They just tacked that name on to get attention. It's about a woman getting out of prison, getting another chance. I'm the woman," she says.

"Well, I'll come, and I'll see to it everybody knows about it, if I have to wear a sandwich board — I did that for pollution," Mr. Toast says.

Colby tugs Ann Lee away. "Are you always so friendly?" he asks her.

"Yes," she says and takes a tray off the stack. She begins to move slowly down the line, stopping to examine each plate and bowl of food, turning the plastic containers of salad to see the other sides. She is not deterred by the frown of the woman at the soup caldron, who waits impatiently, ladle cocked. Finally Ann Lee chooses the special: three chunks of fried chicken, none of them recognizable parts, a pool of yellow corn and a side dish of limas. Colby is afraid she has taken this because it is the special. "I can afford —" he begins, then stops when she smiles.

"I like limas," she says. She takes a glass of buttermilk and walks to a table under a picture of a side-wheeler, brilliantly tinted. Colby follows with a cucumber salad.

"That's all you going to eat?" she asks, diving in.

"I never eat much, I have to watch my weight. I jog," he explains.

"Two troubles I have never had: getting bored and getting fat."

He watches her slash her chicken. Sure enough, the meat is all dark. The tin knife in her hand seems a potent weapon. She picks up a wing and gnaws on it.

Catching his eye, she says, "You're allowed to pick up chicken. Even my prissy aunt in Cincinnati says that."

"It's the way you open your mouth. I can see every tooth in your head."

"All mine," she says. "I like to chew. I like food. I like hot water. I like sex."

He does not take her up on that, prefers to ignore her rashness. Then he feels ashamed for avoiding the flash in her eye. "I guess I rushed in where angels fear to tread," he says, to divert her. "With Grant Tom, I mean. I had the impression he was bullying you."

"Babying me. It comes to the same thing. I'll get my money's worth out of him, don't worry — though it may take some doing." She stops. "I didn't need your help, but I liked it."

"You did?" He is terribly pleased. To disguise that, he stares around the room and sees nothing.

"I don't ask for it — I can take care of myself, I have since I was little. Still, it felt nice." She reaches across the table with her free hand and presses the flat of his arm.

"Oh, Ann Lee" — and he stops, wondering if by some miracle she has now decided what she wants and he is it. "Do you like it here?" he asks her. He notices one of his students in the cafeteria line.

"I haven't paid much attention to it. It'll be fun to see

more of this town. I like seeing more than anything else — just seeing. I guess what finally drove me out of New York was I wasn't seeing much anymore."

"New York!"

"I went to acting school there, two years. It didn't take. I mean, the city didn't."

"You told me you'd never been out of the South."

"Never *lived* out of the South," she amends. "I don't count those two years in New York."

"Why did you come back?"

"Mama needed me, she's not well. Besides, I like the regional theaters. When you do something, the audience appreciates it, they write letters, send flowers, hang around backstage with that look in their eyes, that shine. You only see that in middle-sized towns. Still, I guess you could say I haven't made it in New York, maybe never could make it; I have talent but never have tried too hard to find out where it ends. I would have found out, up there."

She is spooning up corn.

The student from Colby's class comes over and asks a question about a term paper. As he turns his head unwillingly to look at her, Colby sees that it is Andrea Wesker, whom he once took out for a plate of ribs. He introduces her to Ann Lee and watches with amazement as the two women touch hands. It does not seem to him they belong to the same system.

Andrea is wearing her most outrageous blue jeans with a pair of hands stitched on the rear. "I'd like to talk to you," she says ominously, her eyes straying to Ann Lee.

"You know my office hours," Colby mumbles.

"They're no good for me, I have conflicts all those times. Can I see you sometime late this afternoon?"

He agrees in order to get rid of her and watches her switch off, the hands riding.

"What about dessert?" he asks Ann Lee, hoping she has not noticed the special, custard pie, because he wants to rush her through.

"No thank you, I'm fine. I think I've had enough. I'll go out this afternoon, after I get myself settled, and see what the ice cream situation is here; I like peach ice cream a good deal. It's hard to come by, in most places. When I'm rehearsing, peach ice cream keeps me going. Will you take me to the Mayflower?"

He is on his feet before he is aware of the decision to move.

The Mayflower is two blocks from the Rainbow Cafeteria, and Colby wants to walk that distance with Ann Lee beside him. He does not ask her; she does not question; she lets him guide her past the wig stores, the dry fountain crammed with candy wrappers and the defunct delicatessen that was for a while the hope of the mall.

"Each spring, a new hope," he tells her. "Last spring, it was that statue," and he shows her the metal figure of Pan with his pipes, standing on a concrete base that looks like a drinking fountain. "They had water coming out of his pipes till people put bubble gum in them. Nothing works here that's just for decoration, people won't stand for it, they tear it up."

"Things don't usually work that are just for decoration," she says.

Colby hears but does not answer, afraid that she may mean that he is only for decoration. He feels her arm with his right hand, feels the sturdy bone and wants to tell her that he hopes he will never be able to hurt her.

The Mayflower is a small old apartment building, five stories high, with balconies, balustrades and patched green canvas awnings over all the western windows. Colby and Ann Lee go into the lobby, which is empty except for a woman behind a desk. She is expecting Ann Lee and presents her at once with something to sign and a key. She glances once at Colby as though to judge whether he is likely to cause a commotion in the night.

"This is a quiet place," she says. "Many of the elderly."

"I'm quiet," Ann Lee assures her.

"We've had pretty good luck with you theater people. I didn't think so, at first. I said to Fred, 'None of them with their all-night parties.' I guess I had the wrong impression. Grant Tom's mother is my aunt's best friend and so I said I'd give it a try. No problems I have to admit. They grew up together in the old days on South Third. My parents live across the river in Jeffersonville, I've never met Mr. Tom himself although we have had many pleasant telephone conversations. A week in advance, please." She has a small working mouth, Colby notices, and a small wrinkled flat face that is pert and bright. Her hand appears, palm up, doll-sized, on the top of the desk.

Ann Lee pulls a wad of money out of her hip pocket and leafs off bills.

"I thought you said you didn't have any money," Colby protests, trying to make it an aside.

"Grant Tom paid me some in advance."

"That tightwad!" He is immediately suspicious. "I hope at least you gave him a receipt!"

She laughs, and looks at him oddly.

Released by the lady at the desk, they go through a door and climb a flight of stairs. Pale afternoon light flows through a bare and dirty window on the landing. As Ann Lee turns to him, Colby sees for the first time the fine lines beside her mouth. Then she turns back and goes on ahead of him, walking delicately, placing her sneakers one at a time on the steps like a child just learning to climb. Colby chokes off his impulse to put his hand on her buttocks, under the edge of her housewife's cardigan. She is beginning to exist for him, piece by piece, so that now he can say he has visual knowledge of her arm, buttocks, and a slice of ankle between her sneaker and her jeans.

She unlocks the door with a single twist of the key, and a breath of stale cold air billows out. She goes in ahead of him. It is a narrow room. The bed takes up half the space; it is wedged against the wall. There is a yellow dresser with a mirror on top and a straight-backed chair against the window. Through the white curtains, hanging limp, Colby sees the parking lot and the back of the library. The bathroom is a closet with a shower. Next to the door, a folding table is set with a hot plate and a tin percolator.

"It isn't much," he says, dismayed.

"It's fine," she says. "It's clean," she says, and she sits down on the bed, testing it. "A good deal better than I expected."

"It's so small."

"My own room — I don't have to share it. I almost always

have to share. I can come in here and pull down the shade" — and she does so, leaving the room in yellow dimness — "and double-lock the door" — she does so — "and feel safe, alone, warm: take a shower."

She is walking towards the bathroom, letting her cardigan drop, unbuttoning her shirt.

"Take a shower with me," she says, without looking back.

Colby follows behind her on the smooth part of anticipated pleasure which has been closed to him for so many years.

"Why is it so easy with you?"

"Because," she says, "neither one of us has to worry."

There is barely room for one person in the bathroom, and Colby retreats to the bedroom to take off his clothes. He drops each article on the floor, holding it out at arm's length as though he is dropping it from a great height.

He hears the shower turned on and goes to join Ann Lee.

She is standing with her head back, drinking from the shower and allowing the water to stream through her hair. He notices the swallowing motions in her throat which he saw when they first met, and then her broad shoulders and the delicate points of her nipples. Her belly is round above the long curve of her hips, and her knees do not interrupt the straightness of her legs. She is white all over, untouched by the sun. Her pubic hair and the hair under her arms is darker than the hair on her head, more dense and tightly curled. She is turning her toes up in the warm water.

Colby steps in beside her and comes as soon as he touches her bare thigh. The warm water washes his semen away.

She puts her arms around him and rocks him as the water

runs down his shoulders and back. Then she begins to soap him with a green lump of soap, worn down by other tenants. She lifts his arms and soaps under them and runs handfuls of lather over his slack belly, which he contracts, and then down his thighs. Coming up, she cups his penis and balls and soaps them thoroughly.

He is growing hard again, and he takes her there without preliminaries against the warm streaming wall of the shower. Afterwards he takes her again while water streams down her face and through her hair, and each time he comes with a jolt, and there are tears mixed with the water on his face.

Then he wants to climb into bed with her and soothe her with his hands because she has not come, and there seems to be no interval between the wish and the reality. She dries him and turns back the covers. The bed is very narrow but she crawls in beside him and fits into his arms and he feels her long smooth body and begins to grow hard again and thinks this is joy, at last — this woman, Ann Lee, in his arms.

4

FOR SUPPER THAT NIGHT, they go to the Fincastle Deli, a block from the Mayflower. The deli is deserted; it is a lunch place and only stays open in the evening out of lassitude. The girl behind the counter is looking frayed. The hot-food troughs have shreds left in the corners. The girl says there is enough tuna casserole for one helping and enough lasagna for another. Neither looks appetizing in its dried condition, so Colby and Ann Lee fall on the salad bar.

"These salad bars are one of the big changes, since I grew up," Colby says.

He is amazed by the extent and the variety of his appetites. The bowls of lettuce, cucumbers, tomatoes, bacon bits and cheese parings swim in the eye of his imagination, their colors hectic and demanding. He fetches himself a wooden bowl and hands Ann Lee another and they hang over the bar and help themselves to everything. Colby laces his plate with thick pink dressing.

"Pure chemicals," Ann Lee remarks. She is going to eat her salad dry.

They sit down at a table under a plastic Tiffany lamp. Ann

Lee dives into her food with a fork which seems an extension of her hand. Colby watches her and then begins to eat and it seems to him that he has never before earned a clear right to his food.

"I want to tell you what we ate when I was little," he says, launching out, prepared to progress through his life by meals. Ann Lee is encouraging him with a glance, but he also sees that she is chewing her food with concentration.

"At home we used to eat collard greens and fatback and split peas with ham and black-eyed peas and okra, but my mother had a notion that was the kind of food kept people down; I mean, it was the food of the place, that little mountain town." He stops to give Ann Lee a chance to be surprised, then realizes she has no reason to be surprised because he has told her nothing about himself although he feels he has created an atmosphere of some sophistication. He explains, "My father came from Pineville. That was where we lived when I was growing up. My mother came from Lexington, and she believed we would all be kept down in Pineville by that food; we could only be fueled to escape with lamb chops, green peas, mashed potatoes and grapefruit salads."

Ann Lee makes a chewing sound. Colby wonders if she is listening.

"Marrying my father was an act of the imagination," he goes on. "No woman should be expected to live her life at that pitch. He's a mountain lawyer, always on the wrong side, the coal operators' side. Says somebody has to represent them. That's about the lowest thing you can do, in Pineville. He was the one advised the operators how to break strikes, how to avoid paying compensation to some guy's kin when the mine fell in; he's hated more than anybody has any right to be and he thrives on it. Used to say there wasn't a man in the county wouldn't be pleased if he died. If, not when. That was him, too. Is him, too. Beyond mortality. Not beyond morality, though — his kind. He used to say everybody decent got out of Pineville by the time they were eighteen; the ones that stayed behind were just the sludge and ought to be cleaned out of the system."

"What about him?" Ann Lee asks, spearing a crouton.

"Oh, he was the exception."

"Sounds like he slept with a shotgun."

"A pistol under his pillow, next to her pillow, of course — one of those small old double beds so she must have felt that pistol practically next to her cheek. Which amazed me because I knew he had a dream of being gunned down, a man maybe mean but legally innocent — and everybody in Pineville having to admit he died without breaking the law to defend himself. That would be his final glory. So I was surprised he had that pistol; it would have changed the scenario."

"Was your mother proud of him?" Ann Lee stops her chewing, a green bean on her fork.

"She couldn't help but be proud. I mean, he hardly gave her the choice. She used to teach for a while but quit that when they got married. Looked like a robin — plump soft body, feathered, I used to think. Of course she had to seem like she was shocked by him, by some of his doings. And he was rusty-looking. Wore the same black suit all the time, it smelled like coal dust. A yellow-white shirt and a string tie — that was for color — and great big lace-up boots so he could get up to our house — we lived on a hill — or anywhere else, on foot if necessary. He believed cars were made to break down and took no care of his old Pontiac and so it did. I used to tinker with it sometimes and he'd yell, 'Get out of here, boy, that thing ain't meant to run.' He'd been to law school, didn't need to talk that way but knew it made an impression. Rough diamond."

He waits for Ann Lee's comment but does not get one; she is mowing down her lettuce. "Yes, I guess when I think of it my mother was proud of him. She used to laugh at him, though, with her mouth closed, like a pup that's afraid to bark, especially when he was on the telephone giving somebody hell. That was his only hobby — calling up in the middle of the night and giving some editor hell for some kind of a "sentimental distorted . . .' Usually about brave poor families with hogs. He'd call up in the middle of the night and lean back and rock the kitchen chair on its hind legs and cup the receiver under his chin and talk into the air over it, but whoever was on the other end was getting every word because then he didn't sound like any old mountain man, he sounded like pure Virginia gentry — and I can make the same kind of change, I guess." She was still listening and chewing instead of remarking. "And my mother standing behind him and laughing with her mouth closed. . . . Of course they used to fight."

Colby stops. He has not talked about this in years. It takes him back to courting his wife, in Cambridge — three years on the telephone, ending up out of pure fatigue saying the wrong thing, slamming down the receiver in a fit of disgust, then calling back to apologize and start it all over again. "You have no morals," she used to say because he was all the time trying to get her to go to bed.

"Of course they used to fight," Ann Lee says at last, turning up the edges of her cucumbers as though she expects something living to be buried underneath. Then she eats them. "I mean, fighting doesn't necessarily mean anything."

"I used to hear them" — and now, hesitating, he wishes she would put her fork down, concentrate — "big knocking sounds, he'd make those — throwing her against the wall." His voice slows down, he is picking his way among words, trying to find a stopping place. "It got to where I was afraid to look at Mother in the morning, afraid of what I'd see, I mean, he'd hit her with his balled-up fist, one time he broke her nose. You know what those kind of bruises look like? She'd come back from the clinic just as feathered, never did seem to know how to protect herself; I guess it was her laughing he hated and she was never willing to bridle that. That's why I swore I'd get out as soon as I finished school. Get out and never come back. I was their only child and I couldn't protect her. Couldn't even try. She didn't want me to protect her, I guess. Maybe you were right — she enjoyed those fights, some way. People seem to think that. But I felt — getting to be a big boy — I felt it was up to me to stop that business. I never believed she enjoyed it. I'd lie in my bed and listen to those noises and curse myself for a coward. I was afraid of him. I didn't want him to hit me. He used to whip me with his belt. One time when he had me bent over a chair, whipping me, I bit him through the leg of his pants — got a good mouthful of that black coal-dusty mate-

rial but some skin and meat, too. He screamed! That was
when he quit beating me though he claimed it was because
I'd turned twelve. So I always thought if I'd had the strength
of mind to bite him for my mother he might have quit beating up on her, too."

"What happened after you left home?"

"She died six months later. A stroke, or something."

Ann Lee looks at him. "Or something?"

He lets that ride for a while. It irks him for her to come,
so fast, so close to the mark. "She told me when I left it
would kill her."

"They all say that," Ann Lee says promptly. "When I was
ready to light out, Mama told me she never expected to see
me again, and I was just going to Cincinnati. I thought she
meant I wouldn't make it. She thought she meant she
wouldn't make it. Of course we were both wrong. Her first
letter taught me that — she didn't think she could live with
the other kids, alone. I mean, I had helped out."

"I don't mean my going killed her," Colby says. "I mean,
that's ridiculous! Either he killed her or she died the way
they claimed —"

"Killed her!"

"And either way, what difference does it make? She's dead!
You could call it, either way, natural causes. I mean, she'd
put up with him all those years when it was just getting
worse. . . . What could I have done if I'd been there?" He
takes a breath.

"One time when he was beating up on her, I looked at her
and saw her sitting there, all crumpled up and bruised-
looking, and I thought, I'd beat her, too, lam the daylights

out of her every time I saw her sitting there all crumpled up. I look like my father, everybody says I'll get his temper, too, one day, the way I've gotten his dark hair and eyes, and when I saw my mother sitting there, I believed it. It was just a question of time. So I lit out. The one thing I couldn't have stood would have been to hit her."

"Yes," Ann Lee says. "They get that look. That kind of bruised look around the eyes. Fe-male mas-o-chism," she adds, as though she is reading it off a menu.

"I'm glad I didn't have that kind of education," Colby says coldly, reminded of the way his students talk.

"How did you get to college?"

"Scholarship," he says, and imagines Ann Lee picking up some paperback self-help guide about women and love in a Trailways station somewhere. They sell *Jane Eyre* in those places, too, but she would pick up the guide. "Was your dad good to your mother?" he asks, rousing himself to entertain her.

"She was a tough one. She had to raise us with a disabled man. He was a miner, got the black lung, my mother had to go to work. Worked in a diner and raised us, too — on the side, so to speak. Came home from the diner and started dinner and the wash. I'll never forget that — how he would sit. Just sit. One time she tried to get him to do something for her, put patches on some jeans for the boys, and he started to cry. Sat there with the tears running down his cheeks."

"My father would not have represented him if it had come to court."

"Too weak-kneed to try anything like that. He felt, I

guess, it was coming to him; he'd had some years of a pretty good income, married a woman who knew how to manage, and then the black lung, just the way it always happens. All deserved," she adds.

"What kind of masochism do you call that?"

"I call it that kind of man. I mean, he was the one, deep down, thought his bad luck was deserved."

Colby shakes his head. Then he asks suddenly, "You want to come with me someday, visit the old booger? My father?"

"You ought to, anyway, but me . . . I guess. Sure."

"I think you'd be interested."

"Yes," she says, "I'd like to get to know him."

He is horrified by her smile, which reveals two little yellow eyeteeth. Amazing how quickly sympathy can die, he thinks, slashed off at the root. Immediately a swarm of statements wing in. She let me take her to bed too fast. She must let every man who tries. What is she anyway but a runaway mountain girl . . .

"I'll pay for the food," he says.

"No, you won't. Not anymore." She takes a used-looking billfold out of her pocket.

"What are you saying?"

"I make this rule: I pay for myself, in this kind of situation."

"What kind of situation?"

She looks at him. "When I saw it was going to be this way, with me — first one man, then another — I made a couple of rules. You might as well know them, now. One is I always pay for myself after things take this turn."

"Turn?"

"Loving," she says briefly. "After that starts, I always pay for myself. I don't want to muddy the water. Then you should know I don't use those pills or any of those other contraptions. I use rhythm, and if it fails, it fails."

"What?" he cries.

"I mean, I'm always prepared in my mind to have an abortion."

"You mean you didn't have anything . . . You weren't protected, just now?"

She looks at him. "It's my safe time. Otherwise I wouldn't have done a thing." When he continues to gape, she adds, "You're not running much of a risk, Mister. If I get pregnant, I'll take care of it. You'll never be the wiser."

He puts his head down and kisses the back of her hand, which is lying stiffly on the table. Under his lips, he feels the fan of her bones. "I don't mean it that way. I can't stand somehow to think of you not protected."

"I'm careful. Clean and careful." She is still rankling.

"You know, I'm sentimental. I don't like to admit it, but I am. It's hard for me to believe — I guess I don't want to believe — you just . . . just . . ."

She is glaring at him now.

"That it's like this, the way it is for us, for you with other men."

She puts up her hand. "It never is the same."

He tries to swallow this and be satisfied. "You mean it?"

"I don't go looking for it, don't go putting myself in the way of love." He is amazed, now, that she can use the word. "When it comes, in its own time, it's grace. Always. We use the same motions, more or less, speak the same words. Still each time it's a different language."

"Maybe I just don't have your . . . depth of experience. I stay away from women, mainly."

"You were married, weren't you?"

"Yes, but with her — we had gotten it down to a science. I guess that's the way it is with a lot of marriages. The only way we could separate off the disappointment and the anger was to get it down to a science."

"Oh, God," she says.

"Sex gets overrun otherwise with bad feelings."

"Overrun?"

"They would have choked it out. Maybe it should have been choked out — it was just a science but it was functioning. Neither one of us cared much about bed, but we were both too proud to put up with a marriage that didn't have any bed in it."

"How long, since then?"

"Ten years."

"And since then, nobody?"

"Well, of course I've had flings. If you can call those joyless things flings. One girl came and lived with me, in New York. I didn't invite her. She just assumed it was part of the deal. Came one Monday morning with six shopping bags, everything hanging out. I had to pay the taxi. Just shoved herself into my apartment, rearranged the kitchen shelves, put her herb food everywhere, those great big bottles of vitamins, even had the nerve to move my plants around. There wasn't anything I could do to get rid of her. She wouldn't even wash her feet before she went to bed."

Ann Lee laughs. "How long was it before —"

"I got the nerve up to throw her out? Six months. And then I missed her," he admits soberly. "I even missed her horrible little messes. But I learned something. With women, I'm not in a position of control." Colby realizes that although he sounds certain and wise, he's really only now putting this together.

"There must have been some pleasure in it."

"Oh sure. The truth is I'm looking for joy. I know that sounds crazy. I'm ashamed to say it. Maybe the truth is our easy pleasures just cancel out the possibility of joy. Maybe joy only comes in a wasteland. Anyway, I always know I'm going to flunk the pleasure test. Some brand-new shiny girl all panting to be enslaved by the pleasures of the flesh. I'm not sure I have the raw material. I always worry about my stomach. I mean, I jog, but my stomach is middle-aged. I'm always afraid I'll let her down."

"Her?"

"Whoever."

"You didn't let me down," she adds mildly.

"Thank you. . . . They're so clever, these days — you're so clever, these days — it's hard for a man to get away with his in-ad-e-qua-cies." He pronounces the word the way she might, a hyphen between each pair of syllables. "I was impotent a couple of times."

She doesn't say anything.

"And you know, they try so hard to make it up to you. They want to make it up to you so badly. I used to lie there and think I wished they'd let me keep my secret failure, not try to resurrect me, make it all right. I'm a middle-aged man, I have a right to my little failure. Occasionally," he adds.

"You didn't have any of that trouble with me."

He rushes now. "You are . . . so sweet. Your outside is so

competent, you know how to take care of yourself, but inside, in bed, there's this childlike sweetness . . ."

"Don't count too much on that."

He reaches across and takes her hand, wondering how his sympathy has grown its root again, in what fertile soil. He is feeling her again, breathing her again — her freshness, her particular lovely green flavor. "Ann Lee . . ."

She removes her hand after a squeeze. "I've got to go on down to the theater."

Oh God, he thinks, not this, already, this pulling back — don't let her be this way. He realizes that he is still expecting some higher power — unconceived, unnamed — to shape his connection to her.

"Don't pull back," he says.

She does not reply, going through her billfold as though searching for a laundry ticket. Then he realizes she is just counting money. "We better talk," she says.

"Now?"

"It won't alter anything, talk never does."

"I thought you meant you were going to lay down some laws."

"I never do that," she says. "Let sweet Nature take her course."

He does not like Nature with a capital letter and now it is his turn to retreat and he wonders if they have already gotten into a pattern — a step forward and two steps back, swapping roles — and believes that Instant Grat is at the source, that this is what always happens, this premature hardening of lines, when two people have jumped too fast into bed. Either morality or psychology gets you, he thinks

sourly; the punishment is always the same — back into soli-
tude until the next desperate thrust.

"You came, didn't you?" he asks, as though he is filling out
a questionnaire.

"I never do, the first few times. I guess I need to be
friends."

He knows he has only asked this uncouth question to
hamstring what remains of his happiness, and if that is his
aim, he achieves it as he begins to cross-question her. What
does she mean, never the first few times? How many times is
a few? In what circumstances? Does the man (he nearly says,
the partner) make any difference? And anyway, how can she
tell, for sure — he can't tell for sure, even after all this time.
"I mean, all women gasp and wiggle."

"That's enough. This is the worst kind of talk. I don't
know if you want to be jealous or just scientific, but whichever it is, it stinks." She stands up, pushing the table away.
"I'm going to the theater."

Colby is afraid to leave her on this sour note. He imagines
her elaborating it into an entire tune, gone bad. He walks to
the door behind her. "Let me take you down there."

They cross the street and reach the mall, where the wind
is sweeping leaves around the concrete basins. Mr. Toast
with his broom has gone home. A few office workers, waiting for the bus to the East End, stare into the brightly
lighted drugstore windows, where many electrical devices,
mostly orange, are displayed. Colby puts his hands in his
pockets and shivers.

"Don't you ever wear any thick clothes?" she asks, button-
ing her sweater to her chin and hooking a wool scarf over her

head. She looks like a woman who will make it through the tundra.

"Where did you get all that?"

"The theater leftover box. First thing in the morning, I listened to the weather report."

"Don't mother me," he grumbles.

"I was talking about myself!"

"Aren't you trying to set me some kind of example?"

She says, "I never would try to set an example for a man."

Her seriousness makes him silly. "Are we so different?"

"Yes," she says, and begins to walk fast.

"What have I got you haven't got?" he asks — and is immediately sorry.

"We won't talk about that, this time."

They stop in front of the Ten-Cent windows. "When am I going to see you again?" He is ashamed, his hands are tightly curled inside his pockets. "After rehearsal?"

"That'd be pushing it, don't you think? Besides, this'll be my first time to meet the other members of the cast, we might go out for a beer, or something. Call me in the morning, at the theater."

"Aren't you going to get your own phone?"

"Too expensive," she says, "for such a short time." Then she puts out her hand and touches his shoulder.

As he leaves her, Colby remembers his New York therapist talking about Instant Gratification and thinks, Oh God, why did we go to bed so fast, was it really necessary, why didn't we just sit down and have a nice cup of coffee, a nice drink, a nice talk — see you around; OK, then go to her play, probably a lousy actress, maybe take her for a meal sometime, insist on paying, hear about her plans — see you around. None of this wrenching and tearing. Get to know her slowly, by measured degrees — if it seems useful, if it seems appropriate — so that, degree by degree, a graph is drawn, straight lines connecting, he at one end, she at the other, until finally all the lines are connected and then they might go to bed together as a way of placing a point.

Then she never would have seen me shivering like a wet dog.

He knows he has come to a crossing place and he should sit down and start to think about his marriage, women — all that.

He is passing a brightly lit telephone booth. He goes in. It is clean; men don't urinate inside telephone booths in Kentucky, you can use them to get out of the weather. For a while, he thinks he is standing there just to get out of the wind. Then he begins to feel that he should put the telephone to its proper use. Everyone on the mall will be staring at him, at the sight of a lovesick white man trapped like a fish inside a lighted glass tube. He takes out a dime, drops it in and listens to the tinkle. Help is on its way. Without thought or hesitation, he dials I. Weekly's number and Martha tells him to come right over, he is expected, the coffee is on.

5

MARTHA IS STANDING at her kitchen counter. The edge hits the peak of her belly. Amniotic fluid or muscle wall, protect it, Colby prays, seeing the counter edge dent her smock. He remembers her a small woman, bird-boned, he would almost have said inconsequential, but now, nine months gone, she is big, those tiny bones floating somewhere in warm fluid, gases, hot air. Colby has an urge to lay his hands flat on her belly, get down on his knees and lay his head to her navel, which, he has read somewhere, turns inside out in the last stages. He imagines it budding out like a crocus; hastily looks away and addresses I., who is fondling the silent telephone.

"Who are you waiting to hear from?"

"Anita Dent — you know her — child of the golden suburbs come to the university to learn about people she hopes she never has to meet." I. smiles, a little wolfishly, his long teeth crammed into his narrow jaw.

"What's the matter with her?"

"Fallen in love. Her father says, 'Bring that nigger trash home and I'll brain you.' I'm expected to act as go-between."

"I thought you said she never wanted to know —" Colby began.

"Bed is knowing?" Martha interrupts.

"Well, it could be."

Martha says nothing, leaning back to survey her handiwork, a plateful of thick black brownies.

Colby is humbled.

I. says, "I'm not the go-between really, it's just one of my dreams. I mean, she does go out with this colored guy, but for all I know she has no father. She's helping me to get the poetry reading organized. Tomorrow. Eloise Longham is coming down from New York."

"I've heard that name."

"Good poet. Good woman, too. I told her we could guarantee her quite a turnout. I think I mentioned twenty, but Anita got the notice in too late for the paper and we've had to depend on posters and word of mouth." I. unfurls a poster, a muddy rectangle with a green poet face floating in it.

The telephone rings before Colby can find an honest yet tactful reaction, and I., cuddling the receiver, begins to talk rapidly. Martha looks at Colby, grins and raises her eyebrows. Between them passes a silent estimation of Anita Dent, classy as her designer blue jeans with the patches on the knees (and what does she kneel for, Martha might ask), her corduroy hunting jacket, her face with its matched features set between two folds of blond hair.

"She's not the most organized person," Martha says and passes the plate of brownies.

I. takes one, crumbles it and mouths a bit while continuing his monologue into the telephone.

"I met somebody," Colby says, to the air.

Martha begins to scrub out the brownie pan and then turns off the water and stands listening, looking at Colby over her shoulder.

"I mean, a girl. A woman. She was hitchhiking, yesterday. I picked her up. I had supper with her tonight." He snaps up a brownie and crams it in his mouth.

"At long last!" Martha says. "I thought for a while there it would never happen."

"It's just a girl," Colby says gloomily.

"You have that look in your eyes!"

To avoid her appraisal, he looks around the kitchen at the blue gingham curtains, the geraniums, the pots hanging on the wall. Martha moves around so that she catches his eye, at last, and says, "Now Colby, 'fess up."

Swallowing hard, he tastes tears and wishes he could tell her humorously yet discreetly how Ann Lee felt in bed — the smoothness and ease which have already lost their details, becoming a mist, an enveloping warm cloud. Recounting it to Martha — if that could be done — might re-create it.

She says, "You've already been to bed with her."

"You never were that quick before you got pregnant."

"All the senses enlarged. I know the look you get when you're satisfied. It's pretty close to the look you have when you've just finished a leg of my lemon chicken."

I. hangs up the phone, sighs and says, "Anita's distressed. She feels she's let me down."

"She has," Martha says, and goes back to scrubbing the pan.

"Eloise Longham is not actually going to be counting heads," I. says, to persuade himself. "She's much more interested in her creature comforts. Says she must have breakfast in bed at the motel. What do you think, honey?"

"If I don't go into labor tomorrow, I'll pack her a care basket — hot thermos of coffee, a roll. I don't know if that would do her but it's the best I can manage." Martha moves to a chair, poises herself, then drops into it, spreading her knees.

"Probably not, but I don't see the alternative," I. says, watching his wife with interest.

Colby asks, "Are you planning on going into labor tomorrow?"

"I'm two weeks overdue. I've started to get twinges in the perineal area," Martha says, patting her belly. The soft slapping reminds Colby of Ann Lee patting her flat stomach, after lunch, and he is restored to one detail. "Col's met somebody, a girl," Martha tells I.

"That's nice. Will she come to the reading?"

"I don't know if she likes poetry. I don't know much about her education. She comes from Cincinnati or the mountains, I'm not sure which, there seems to be some question in her mind."

Martha folds her hands, etches a cuticle. "Do you have fun with her?"

"I don't know if that's what I —"

"The trouble with you, Col, is you never have fun with girls. Or women. Hard work, maybe, exercise, something like that, but no fun!"

Colby wants to ask her if she has fun, bouncing like a lead balloon on I.'s prick.

I. is busy writing something down on a list but he asks,

"Cathy Hardy, the girl you met at the museum, that one in class — is there anybody else?"

"I like my own company!"

"That's it!" Martha says. "You enjoy yourself too much, alone, you'll never have that kind of fun with anybody else."

"Now don't talk dirty," I. says.

"I may deserve happiness, but I know I don't deserve fun," Colby says to her screech.

"Does the toad under his stone deserve the morning light?" I. asks. "That's the first line from one of Eloise's poems, one of her best, I think."

"I thought it was only women had to deserve things," Martha says. "Did your ex-wife deserve you?" She spreads her thighs a little wider as though to ease herself, and Colby is daunted.

"I don't know that I had much to offer, then; I didn't really have my act together." He fears that he has put that phrase in quotation marks.

I. is busy with his list. "We'll pick up Eloise at the airport and bring her here for supper, before the reading."

"As long as I'm not in the hospital." Martha leans towards Colby. "Did she love you? Your wife?"

"That's not in my vocabulary. We cared about each other."

"Oh, God," Martha says.

I., alerted at last, looks at her. "When we met, you wouldn't talk about anything except caring. Mutual caring, at that. I never knew there was another kind."

"That's long in the past." Martha tosses her head. There is not enough hair on it to make an impression.

Colby smiles. "Now listen," he says, seizing the upper hands, "she — my wife — was a Radcliffe Ph.D. with a lot of money —"

"I know all that."

"And a father who brought her up literally on his knee. I mean, what do you expect of me? Her mother died young, the two of them just had each other. I used to think it would have been better for her if they had just gone on and —"

"Fucked?" Martha inquires.

I. says, "You are always putting words in this man's mouth."

Colby goes right on. "He — her father, the old professor — he gave her her start in the English Department, and he gave me my start in the English Department, too. Nicely arranged so we wouldn't compete. You know I never would have gotten anywhere at Harvard without that; my Kentucky accent didn't help. But he — Professor McKee, I never called him anything else — he was chairman of the English Department and so . . . We lived the first three years we were married underneath him on Garden Street, and my office was under his office — he could even hear my phone ring. It was no more and no less than I deserved. I didn't grow up. Now quit looking that way. I went there on scholarship, I never had much polish or confidence. My wife helped me some with that . . . I needed it. Her help, I mean. Besides, we cared about each other — those are the correct words," he adds, in a lower voice. "The winter day we walked around the pond in Concord and she said she'd marry me — I thought I'd made my life. I mean, compatible careers, and all. Besides, you should have seen her on her bike. She flew.

She had that privileged way of getting over obstacles as though they didn't exist — and grace, and charm, and energy. I mean, what could I do with all that?"

I. says, "I have a feeling you are shortchanging yourself."

"Well, I wanted her life."

"Southern boy makes good," Martha says. "What's so terrible about that?"

"I'm not ashamed of it, not anymore," Colby agrees. "I always had to make my own way, even inside that setup. The first time Professor McKee invited me to dinner — a small omelet, he didn't claim to be much of a cook . . . We cared about each other," he repeats, having lost the thread.

Martha asks, "Why did it go wrong, beginning so small?"

"She was part of the whole arrangement. I think it was that. When I started to hate teaching there, hate those faces — too much ruckus and carrying on, too little respect . . . I guess she fell through with the rest of my life. Laura always thought she was on the side of the revolution, she'd led that kind of privileged life. I knew I was just trying to teach them something about Melville. Then, I wanted to move and she couldn't live apart from her father or Cambridge, didn't even want to try New York. She was teaching a course on nineteenth-century women poets . . . It was also Sunday night supper with her father, his very delicate stew, you'd hardly know there was meat . . .

"And then when I finally left and came back here, I knew I'd lost my flying start . . .

"We cared about each other," he says for the third time, acknowledging now that he will never know whether it was love. It was never tried in the furnace. Still he can't stop talking although he is no longer sure that either of the Weeklys is listening. "When I first saw her, I knew who she was, everyone knew who she was, she just finished playing the girl who has her hands hacked off and her tongue cut out in *Titus*. Everything depended on her eyes. Brown eyes, thick long lashes. I knew who she was, but even if I hadn't, I would have followed her, weaving on her bike through the traffic on Brattle Street as though she was riding sidesaddle, her stockings with a peacock-feather pattern."

Martha applies her hands to the sides of her belly and concentrates. Then she says, "I., give me your watch."

I. unhooks the silver chain which attaches the pocket watch to his blue jean belt loop and slides the watch on it back across the table. It skids, lands in Martha's lap. She takes it and tilts its face up to the light.

"She didn't want me to leave her, in the end," Colby goes on, looking at Martha's hand applied to the side of her stomach. "She cried. She sat on our bed and cried and made gestures with her hands as though she was going to pull out her hair. 'I am going to tear my hair,' my mother used to say but she never even lifted her hands. I thought my wife would die without me, I thought she wouldn't be able to get up in the morning, but with Valium and two months of therapy, she went right on, she found herself an assistant professor in no time."

Martha has transferred the watch to the palm of her right hand; she looks at its face, closes her fingers over it, leans back hard against the back of the kitchen chair and stares at the ceiling.

"She told me once she would die without me but the

strange fact was I nearly died without her," Colby goes on. "I was determined not to take care of myself, I lost fifteen pounds."

Martha places the watch on the kitchen table. "One time when we went over to your place —"

"The fern farm," I. says.

Colby says, "That dump!"

"— there wasn't anything in the icebox except some bamboo sprouts and an old cantaloupe, half eaten, there was nothing in the drainer except a week's supply of coffee cups, rinsed out, I admit. You were eating at the Handy Andy on the corner of Bardstown Road, complaining about the junk food and doing nothing about it — they didn't even have a sanitary certificate, at that time."

"I'd just been here a week. You started bringing me bean soup and bread."

"The good things I make for I."

I. grins.

"You must wonder why I stopped bringing you food," Martha says.

"No, I don't wonder," Colby says quickly, but it is too late.

"I knew you'd never start to take care of yourself as long as I spoiled you."

"You're what got me started! Taking care of myself, I mean. I'm jogging five miles a day."

"And then I introduced you to the Healthy Noodle," I. reminds him, "and you started to think twice about meat."

Colby says, "I'm still thinking but I do eat it sometimes."

"You could eat twice a day at the Healthy Noodle and have a different vegetable plate every time," I. reminds him.

Martha picks up the pocket watch, checks it, holds it in her hand, leans back against the chair back and stares at the ceiling.

Colby says, "I do lose weight on that diet. I'm in good shape, if I say so myself. It's about time for something to happen to me. I've been working to get myself into decent shape. I jog seven days a week, in the rain, even, the park full of leaves and damp . . ." He rocks back in his chair and slaps his flat thighs. It occurs to him that Ann Lee possibly admired his thighs, when they were in the shower.

Martha gasps. The two men look at her.

"Five minutes apart," she says.

I. is staring with surprise and Colby is asking, "What? What?"

"I think you better call young Dr. Malone," Martha tells I. "I'm too old to sit here and amuse myself."

I. springs at the telephone.

Colby looks at her. She is changing in front of his eyes, swelling, as though by sheer force of mass she is about to fill the room. He remembers a fairy tale about a magic cake that swelled out of all proportion, filling the oven, then the kitchen, then the whole house, finally blowing off the roof. He remembers the palely tinted picture of the roof flying through the air, sideways, like a sail.

I. is apologizing into the telephone; he has dialed wrong; he cannot seem to hang up. *"Non, non, je veux pas parler—"*

"Hang up!" Martha orders. She seizes the watch again, holds it cupped fiercely in her right hand, knots her face, presses her feet against the floor and begins to pant like a dog.

"Get the doctor!" Colby yells, snatching the telephone from I., punching buttons.

I. takes the phone back and finally gets the doctor. He wants Martha in the hospital right away. Because of her age, she is a high-risk primapara, a term Colby hopes he will never have to hear again.

The two men get her up, unaware that she is in the middle of a contraction. She flaps her hand at them — "Wait! Wait!" — panting through the words. As they propel her towards the doorway, she droops, licks her lips, closes her mouth. "All right, now." She smiles at Colby.

They are walking down the path to the car, stumbling in the beam from the porch light, when she stops, places her feet wide apart and groans.

I. rubs her back round and round with the palms of both his hands.

Water rushes down her legs, spills onto the path, pools and runs off between the pebbles.

"God!" Colby exclaims. He is clutching his hair.

Then she is Martha again. "That's good. The waters broke." She steps over the puddle and goes down the path to the car.

As I. helps her into the front seat, she asks Colby to go back to the house for her purse.

He runs up the path, slams into the house. In the kitchen, the burner is still on under the coffee; he turns it off. Then he runs around the house, nosing for her purse, finds it at last on a windowsill in the hall, behind a pot of dried grasses. The purse feels creased, like the ear of a small domestic animal. He grabs it and runs. In the living room, the heterogeneous collection of sofas and armchairs seems like a herd, already waiting for her return. He thinks with a gush of bitterness that this is her house, that I. really has no part in it, any more than I. has in the upheaval of her body, and he re-members the house on Garden Street, the kitchen window crowded with herbs, his wife's bottles in the bathroom — the way women take over spaces.

Rushing to the car, he skirts the puddle and groans at his own fastidiousness.

They are waiting for him, the engine running. He sees I.'s face staring out the window. "Where were you all this time? Get in!"

"You want me to go with you?"

"Get in!" I. bawls.

Martha, sitting in the front seat, is frozen in a contraction.

Colby darts into the backseat, bangs the door, drops the purse over into Martha's lap. She does not acknowledge it, she is lost, I.'s watch clutched in her hand. As the contrac-tion passes, she pats the purse and nods at Colby.

Suddenly Colby remembers her on the beach at the lake at Natural Bridge, remembers her running along the edge of the brown water, her hair tied up with a piece of string. She was big, then, but not handicapped, the skirt of her mater-nity number covered most of it. Later that month, he re-members her making raspberry jam, humming away over her boiling pots; how healthy she looked, how Colby cared for her and envied I. for finding such a wife, I. who needed and could accept her care. Colby saw him once kneeling be-side her, his head in her lap, while she slowly brushed his thin hair.

Now he hears her whining like a whipped dog.

Colby leans over the seat and talks rapidly. "Laura and I never had children, never wanted children, it didn't occur to either of us because we were both only children. We never knew family depends on the number of people in it . . ." She is whining over his words now, a thin whine — wind in high-tension wires.

He wants to lean over the seat and cram both hands in her mouth.

I. is hunched over the steering wheel, driving slowly, barely accelerating to make the hill, creeping out into the heavy traffic on Bardstown Road.

"Which hospital is it?" Colby asks.

"Baptist," I. says.

"You're coming with me to the labor room," Martha says in her ordinary voice.

I. does not answer, he is threading a hole between a truck and a camper, leaning on the steering wheel.

"You're coming to the labor room," she repeats in a whisper because another contraction is beginning and she forces her feet against the floor, then tries to relax, pants. The pants are the worst, for Colby; he thinks he can smell her sour breath. Still, he leans forward and massages her shoulders, thin under her smock; she leans back against the seat and he smells her damp hair.

He goes on rubbing with both hands, shifting his grip on her shoulders, wishing he knew how to do it right. Now and then she groans.

"There has been so little love in my life," Colby says as though this will distract them. "A lot of satisfaction seeking, pleasure seeking, but so little love . . ."

"Given, or received?" Martha asks in her ordinary voice.

"I never could feel it," Colby says, rubbing hard with both

thumbs. "That doesn't mean, of course, that I wasn't being given it. . . . Giving — I never did that, I was always too hungry. My poor wife used to say I was feeding off her bones."

"Oh God, Colby, shut up, it's starting again," Martha whispers, and then she begins to hum. I. speeds up suddenly, passing a truck, veering off into a dimly lighted side street. Colby sees the vacant eyes of stripped buildings. "This will be quicker," I. says. Colby is rubbing faster, now, trying to keep pace with her hum.

"I thought they said first babies came slow!" he bursts out.

They are flying through side streets of lit-up shotgun houses, and Colby tries to believe that each of these houses has witnessed at least one birth. Men have sat in outer rooms, listening through doors, or rushed off for the doctor; men have stood idle in their own kitchens while granny women heated water, men have stuffed fingers in their ears to block out screams. Can there be a connection, he wonders, rubbing harder and harder, feeling the heat he is generating in the thin synthetic material, between the helplessness of men waiting for the birth of their children and the thinness of their connection with those children, later on? He is glad to seize on a thought. Where there is no role, can there be a connection? Who remembers the night of the conception?

"You're rubbing too hard," Martha says, shifting her shoulders away from his hands and he leans forward and kisses her reeking hair.

I. with sudden competence darts down a ramp and they are under the bulk of the hospital.

As they stop, Colby leaps out and shouts at two orderlies, who come hurrying with a stretcher on wheels. I. sits behind the steering wheel as though stunned, and Martha, between contractions, is staring straight ahead. The orderlies open the car door and scoop her out. They hoist her onto the stretcher and smooth a sheet over her. I. is still sitting under the steering wheel staring, and Martha calls as they roll her away, "I., you're coming to the labor room with me, not the delivery room, the labor room, you're coming with me . . ."

"We've got to park," Colby says as he gets into the front seat.

I. presses his foot down slowly on the accelerator. The car inches along. Colby realizes he is not headed in any particular direction.

"All right," he says. "Stop!"

I. stops.

"Where are we going?" Colby asks.

"I told her I'd go to the labor room with her," I. says. "I said, 'Not the delivery room, the class didn't prepare me for that.' We compromised on the labor room."

"We should park so you can go back."

A car, waiting behind them, honks and forces I. to drive on. At last they find a slot at the curb and I. slides the car in. He turns off the motor and leans his forehead on the steering wheel. "I don't want to go back there, Col."

"Don't go, then."

"If she had a mother, alive . . . If she had a sister . . ."

Colby takes a tissue out of the box on the dashboard and hands it over.

"She's not on good terms with any woman . . ."

They stare at each other.

"I never could do anything for my wife," Colby says. "Even in bed, I never could do anything for her. Why can't we do anything for them, except make them —"

"No," I. interrupts. "I love her. She knows that. It doesn't have to be proved." He wipes his face with the tissue. "Let's get away from here, Col, we can't do anything. That class was a fraud, it was all giggles and breathing exercises, you saw the kind of pain . . . We can't do anything. She'll understand."

"Like hell she will," Colby says stoutly. "We're going in."

They step through the emergency room door and are lost for a few minutes in a swirling current. Two nurses are sitting at a table, writing things down.

I. accosts one and is promptly reprimanded; it seems they are in the wrong place. I. turns, heads out the door and runs for another entrance. Colby is hurrying along behind. He is almost certain now that I. has forgotten him.

They come to another desk where a nurse sits, and I. explains, "I have to get to the labor room, my wife is waiting for me."

"That requires written permission from your doctor," the nurse says, looking at them.

I. rummages through his pockets and comes up with a scrap of paper. The nurse glances at it, then slides a sheet of paper across the table to I. He stares at it. Colby, looking over his shoulder, sees that it is a release and prods I. to sign it. He does. Then he is off, winging towards the elevator.

"Not you, sir!" the nurse calls after Colby.

Colby knows there is no use arguing. He turns back, deflated.

"You can get a cup of coffee in the waiting room," the nurse says, adding, "There are magazines . . ."

He turns, walks a few paces, sits in the appointed place, sees a lamp shining at his elbow, a patch of bristling rug at his feet. On the other couch, a man is sitting with a briefcase open on his knees. Colby picks up a magazine and stares at the cover.

After a while, the man with the briefcase snaps its lid and stands up.

"I tell you, they expect us to put up with a lot . . ."

"I'm not the father," Colby says.

"I mean, it would be different if there was something we could do . . . Uncle? Friend?"

"Friend," Colby says.

6

"WELL, IT'S A GIRL," Colby announces when he meets Ann Lee in the Fincastle Deli at nine the next morning. He called her early, waking her, because he has a ten o'clock class, which he cannot face without seeing her first.

Ann Lee holds up a forkful of scrambled eggs in a salute. "A girl!"

"Eight pounds, six ounces, I. says a lot of black hair."

"He stayed with her the whole time?"

Scornful now of her suspicions, Colby slabs butter on his toast and says, "Of course he stayed with her. Dr. Malone gave him a white gown and a mask and those blue paper slippers and I. stood beside Martha and rubbed her back the whole time."

"In the delivery room?"

"Certainly!"

"They let her sit up?"

Colby has not yet pictured it in his mind.

Ann Lee goes on, "Ordinarily, they don't let laboring women sit up, they make them lie on their backs, the worst position."

"How do you know that?"

"I worked for five years in the mountains with an outfit that delivers babies."

"When was that?"

"Some time ago. I left because I needed to make more money. They thought the experience was pay enough, and they were nearly right. I was up every morning at six, winter and summer, mucking out the stalls, saddling for the midwives. I liked that."

"I don't know actually if they let Martha sit up," Colby finally confesses.

"You and your wife never had any kids?"

He is insulted by her short memory.

"Why not?" she asks, sinking her teeth into a muffin.

"It just never seemed very appealing."

"Well, I'm one of four, and it was always clear to me that we were what held them together — my parents, I mean."

"Maybe we didn't want to be held together."

"What about now?"

"I'm divorced," he reminds her.

"Don't you want to be held together with me?" she asks, perfectly serious.

"What are you talking about? We just met!"

"I was just wondering if you are serious." She takes another generous bite of her muffin.

Colby lays down his fork. "What a question!"

"It seemed like you were serious, in bed."

He knows that he cannot frighten her away from her perception so he says, "I'm always serious, in bed."

She nods. "I thought so."

"Why so sad?"

"Not sad. It seems we have to do things differently."

He feels a bone chill. "Differently?"

"We can't go to bed together if you're serious."

"What?" He nearly leaps out of his chair.

"It was playing, before. Now it wouldn't be playing."

"Are you crazy? I said I was always —"

"If you're serious, we can't play. We might mess each other up. We have to wait and see how it's going to turn out."

Her authority daunts him, enrages him. "How come you know so much?" he snarls.

"Look, Mister, I've been living on my own since I was fifteen years old. I'm not the kind of woman men don't see. It comes to this, now and then," she says, beckoning to the waitress and asking for another cup of coffee. Even in his agitation, Colby notices the way the two women smile at each other. "This is my last cup of coffee for today," she explains. "Grant Tom doesn't like me to drink too much."

Colby wants to scream at the detour but manages to restrain himself enough to say, "You mean we are just going to be friends?"

"I wouldn't say that, I think that would be kind of foolish. What about lovers? Waiting lovers." Then, seeing that he is enraged and hurt, she adds, "I'm going to be here such a short time, Col. How would you feel when I left if we'd spent every night together?"

He says crossly, "I wasn't counting on every."

"Well, I might get to count on it. We'd be like married for a while, that's what happens right off when you're serious, and then we'd make all kinds of plans to meet somewhere, sometime, and then things would come up and we'd start to be afraid and after a few months of never seeing each other and trying to talk on the telephone, we'd start to ruin the whole thing in our minds. No. We wait till we see what's going to happen. You don't even know whether I have any talent," she adds, smiling.

"What has that got to do with it?"

"A lot. I'd like to come and see you sometime, in class. See you? Hear you?"

"Both. OK." The terrible oppression lifts a little. "When will you come?"

"We're rehearsing pretty solid the next few days, but we'll have a break over the weekend. We'll work it out. Listen, I need to find someplace else to stay, the Mayflower's more than I'm willing to spend."

"I thought you knew yesterday —"

"I didn't know yesterday what Grant Tom was going to pay me. I found out last night."

"So it is the minimum."

"Yes," she says calmly.

"That's terrible!" But she will not be drawn into agreeing with him.

"They're getting along on a shoestring," she says. "Will you help me find someplace else to stay?"

"Yes, I will," he says, crushing visions of her curled up in his single bed. After all, he thinks, he would be ashamed of his dismal apartment, seen through her eyes, the stale smells, the crumpled sheets. There is an advantage to be found in any reversal. "You any good with babies?" he asks, thinking fast.

"I told you, five years in the mountains: I had some experience, then."

"I'll see what I can do." The last of his anger is fading.

"I certainly would be obliged . . ." She is wiping her plate with a piece of bread.

"Would you go with me tonight to hear some poems?" he asks.

"We have the evening off. What time?" She is looking around for the check.

He tries not to think what he would have felt if she'd said she was busy. "I'll pick you up at the Mayflower at eight."

"All right," she says, and takes the check, studying it to see how much she owes. Colby counts it a victory when she lets him leave the tip.

He goes directly from her to the hospital. He needs to talk to Martha about his dilemma. She is sitting up in bed when he goes into her room, wearing a pink jacket of some kind — he has never seen her in nightclothes before, or in pink. The baby is lying in a box attached to the foot of her bed.

Colby, out of politeness, leans down to study the baby. The nose and mouth are crushed together on top of the chin, under a long slope of forehead. He wonders whether this is some kind of temporary deformity, whether the features will rise in time and occupy the rest of the face. He does not ask; for all he knows, Martha thinks it is beautiful.

On the way, he bought Martha a bunch of white daisies, the first flowers he has bought in years, which seem to place him in a courtier's position. So he is embarrassed to find himself talking almost at once about Ann Lee.

"What's gone wrong so soon?" Martha asks after his first sentences.

"She has some problems about . . . intimacy," he mumbles.

"That's too bad," Martha says, but she is not really listening; she is shifting herself awkwardly in bed. "I'm sorry, Col; I'm uncomfortable from the stitches."

He is surprised. She is looking so much herself, except for the pink jacket, that he expected her to listen to him exactly as she always listens in her own kitchen.

"Can I do anything for you?" he asks uneasily.

"Would you get me that rubber pillow?"

He reaches for it gingerly. It is a heart-shaped inflated ring. "What do I do with it?"

"Just put it under my rear end." She is hoisting herself up on her arms.

Unwilling to refuse her, he turns down the bedcovers and sees her thick, straining white thighs and nearly shouts at her, "Hey, you've got the wrong one, wait for I." Instead he shoots the pillow in and hears the dull sound of escaping air as she sits on it.

"Now maybe I'll be able to listen to you," she says.

Colby has nothing more to say.

"What's wrong?" Martha says.

"Here you just had a baby, you're in pain, you must want to talk about that . . ."

She does. He listens at first. She is singing a hymn of praise. For Colby the hymn is flawed by the graphic words she uses. At each of these words, he blanks, his ears go dead, he becomes a smiling receiver that does not receive. Cervix.

Placenta. Perineum. Episiotomy. Outside the window, the sky is blue and gold, the park trees are tipped with red, and Colby turns to rest his eyes on the beautiful neutrality of nature. After a while, Martha stops talking.

"You don't want to hear this, do you?"

"I'm sorry. My wife . . . My ex-wife . . . She had an abortion, once. Didn't tell me about it till afterwards and then treated me to every detail." His voice is struggling. "I can't understand anything like that. Those are not my terms."

" 'For Celia, Celia, Celia shits!' "

Shamed, he is silent, he looks at the floor, at the crisscrossed scrubbed linoleum.

"What can I do?" Martha asks, relenting.

"Ann Lee needs a place to stay." As Colby says it, he looks carefully at Martha's left ear, singling it out for attention. "She can't afford to stay at the Mayflower. She says she's good with babies, she used to work with the midwives up in the mountains."

Martha looks surprised. Then she begins to consider. Colby sees that she is considering calmly, with no sense of rush or pressure, and he begins to relax.

"We do have the extra bedroom at the back," Martha says, ruminating. "You mean she would help me out with the baby in exchange for room and board?"

"Yes."

"How would that help you?"

He hesitates. "Well, I think it would prevent her from sort of disappearing."

Martha smiles. "Maybe. I'm nursing the baby, she wouldn't have to get up at night, but she could do a little cooking —

if I can stand to hand over my kitchen — run errands, answer the phone, things like that."

"Will you take her?"

"You really want it badly?"

Colby says, "I think I just want the three of you to be together."

"I don't understand."

"I guess I don't understand, either. My first marriage —"

"First?"

"And last! It was a group. I mean, I liked her father, admired him — more than I did her. I wanted to be a part of the life they had together. Sometimes I think that's the only way it works. It wasn't just Laura. She realized that, finally, it helped to bring on the end. The way her father held the carving knife at Sunday supper, then laid it down on a special ivory-and-silver holder. I don't mean I'm a snob, it's just there was some continuity there — doing the same things, in the same way. Caring for people becomes part of that pattern — I feel that when I see you kneading bread."

"Every Monday. Tuesday it's cookies and Wednesday's the day I iron and mend."

"Country woman," he says, grinning. "Who ever heard of living that way anymore?"

"It feels suitable to me."

"She's a real country woman — Ann Lee. I guess I also want you to reinforce that in her." Suddenly he leans down and lays his cheek on the crisp-smelling sheet next to her square hard-worked hand. "I love you — the three of you — I can't divide one out . . ."

"You mean I. and me and the baby?"

"No!"

"I haven't even met this girl of yours."

"You'll meet her tonight, at the poetry reading. I mean, I. will meet her."

"Yes, I don't believe I'm quite up to that. Well, I guess I would take in a stray cat."

He yelps, "She's not a stray."

"I'm sorry, Col. I want to meet her." Then she is reaching for the baby, who is beginning to twist and mew. "I'm going to nurse her now. I have a feeling you won't want to see that."

"I've never seen that." His enthusiasm is thin.

"Leave, Col, get a cup of coffee, something to eat. You look like a ghost."

Walking down the corridor, Colby carefully avoids the women floating by in nightgowns and remembers his mother saying, "Pride cometh, Colby. Pride cometh before a fall."

He drives straight to his ten o'clock class. He is still distracted, and so the hour is a little more leaden than usual. He has just finished talking about "The Birthmark" when Andrea Wesker raises her hand. Colby dreads her question. "Doesn't it mean he has to accept the way she is? That's love?"

He shakes his head. "That wasn't what I meant."

She waits, tilting her luxuriant head of hair so that a few carefully shaped blond tendrils spill across her white blouse.

"It's about eternal damnation," Colby says.

The class does not stir.

"Eternal damnation? I thought it was about love."

"The same thing."

The class laughs halfheartedly.

He goes on, "The birthmark is the mark of her personality, the unique thing about her. If he can remove the mark, he makes her perfect, and neutral, he removes the secret of her identity."

Andrea is writing. The bell rings, the others rise and begin to gather up their things. Colby is still not keen on looking any of them in the eyes and he busies himself with his papers.

"Eternal damnation —?" Andrea asks.

"Not to be able to love what's real."

Andrea is not going to let him off so easily. She sidles up to the desk, timing her arrival: the last of the other students has reached the door.

"It seems so sad," she says.

"Hawthorne is a great realist." He wonders if he will sound so pontifical when he is genuinely old. Her talcum-powder smell disturbs him and he turns towards the door.

"I mean, I thought there was like hope in that story. She really does care about him, don't you think?"

"I think you're going at it the wrong way, you're approaching it like some true-life romance. Hawthorne doesn't care about romance."

She says stubbornly, "I still think it's about marriage. Living together. I still think it's a little like 'The Wedding Journey.'"

He tries to make the leap and fails.

"It's about people living together, after all," she insists.

"Look, I've got to go now," he says. "I haven't been feeling very well lately."

"I liked it when you took me out for those ribs," she says sadly.

"Andrea, you need a boyfriend."

"How do you know what I need?"

He has no answer.

"You turn me down without even knowing who I am!"

He knows he is being pressed towards a small corner but also that she does not have the power to press him all the way. He wants to protect her from the disappointments she is so clever at accumulating, from the snowfall of unhappiness which will bury the rest of her life.

"You have every right to want a boyfriend, there's nothing wrong with that, what could be more normal, an attractive girl like you . . ." He runs down, realizing that she does not attract him although he can estimate the way she might attract other men, can add up her good points and come to an objective conclusion.

Then he is chilled by the realization that almost no one in the world attracts him, either physically or intellectually, they are all too graphic, too real, they lack the mistiness, they take up space. He goes on bitterly, "You just want somebody to take you to the movies, fill your life, take you out to eat —"

"Ribs," she says, through falling tears.

"I can't do that for you, I'm not made that way, I don't like anybody well enough. Mainly I want to be alone."

"What kind of a girl —" She stops, then adds, "You're in

love, I can tell, why didn't you tell me that from the beginning, why did you tell me all those other lies?"

"Not lies." He offers her a box of tissues, watches her blow her nose and knows that she will survive.

"I've got to go now," he says and leaves her standing beside his desk, her hands full of tissues, blowing and blowing.

7

ELOISE LONGHAM stands poised behind a lectern in a room under the library. It is a windowless room, small, with several buzzing fluorescent tubes set in the acoustical-tiled ceiling; the walls are lined with bookcases, on top of which sit white plaster busts of poets and composers. Eloise is a thin middle-aged woman, wearing a long loose purple dress; Colby thinks she has the afterglow, now quite faded, of a woman who has been loved early, given an early start. He remembers I. saying she had a poem published in *Partisan Review* when she was eighteen and was for several years the mistress of a distinguished older poet.

She leans forward on long forearms to survey the crowd. It cannot really be called a crowd, yet it is a large gathering for a poetry reading. The Indian student from I.'s romantic poetry course is sitting on a folding chair next to the door; he has the origami look of a paper thing about to fly. In front of him, Andrea Wesker and her sidekick, a lovely little blond who has never been known to say a word, are perched like birds on a wire. Another of I.'s colleagues who has left teaching to devote himself to rehabilitating houses in the old sec-

tion of town sits or rather squats on his heels near the door.
Then there are five people Colby doesn't recognize and an elderly secretary from the English Department. The little room
is nicely arranged with people; there are no large spaces between them yet there is no sense of crowding.

"Shall I begin?" Eloise asks I., and he gestures to her to
wait one more second while he checks the hall for stragglers.

Ann Lee is sitting condensed on a chair next to Colby; he
realizes that they have never been part of a group before.

"How do you like it?" he asks, under his breath.

"How do I know? It hasn't begun yet."

"I mean, the room. The crowd."

She looks around at the shelves of poetry, the white busts.
"It's calm. I guess that's what it's supposed to be." She sounds,
for her, uncertain.

Colby wishes he had fed her, first; he feels some diminu-
tion in her current of energy. She was late finishing rehearsal
and Colby, barred by Grant Tom, paced the velvet corridor,
listening to her voice. She came out finally, looking pale.
They had a little talk, in the car. She is paired with a young
fool of a leading man; he plays a prison guard who falls in
love with his prisoner, but he is not able to bring the necessary range or force to the part, he makes the lines sound
ridiculous, and the author, a young woman who has never
written another play, is reduced to tears regularly by his per-
formance. Colby heard all this in the car on the way to the
campus, and when he broke in to offer a pizza, Ann Lee, looking strained, not paying attention, told him she wouldn't be
able to keep a thing in her stomach.

Colby sighs, feeling overwhelmed by his concerns. He is

watching I., who comes back to report that there are no stragglers in the hall.

"Then I will begin." Eloise Longham holds up her hands and shakes them so that her long loose sleeves slide back. Her arms are surprisingly white and round. She lifts her chin. As she begins to read, Colby ceases to feel sorry for her.

> "Pacing the beach at break of day,
> I saw the barren stoat
> Efface his shadow on the clay
> And stride across the mote —"

Ann Lee leans forward, elbows on her knees. Her breath moves the hair at the sides of her face, lifting pale threads. Colby tries to believe that he will never touch her again.

At the end of the poem, there is a small shower of applause. Eloise Longham looks up, her eyes moving rapidly from face to face.

I. says, "Lovely." His voice is full of care.

Eloise places the first poem at the bottom of her pile and pulls out another as though at random. It is a woman speaking of her daughter, a woman wrapped in the desolation and the pride of loss:

> "She will sleep here tonight
> Though this is not her room;
> She will sleep here as a concession
> To my despair."

Colby thinks, We are in this together, this desolation of failed hopes. He admires the courage in this faded woman, which causes her to take this absurd risk, riding a plane from New York to stand in front of a handful of strangers.

"Poems . . . Yet men die for the lack of them," he whispers to Ann Lee.

She is cut off from him now, leaning forward, listening to this woman speak about pain.

When it is over, Eloise falls back from the lectern, and Colby sees the sweat on her face. I. stands up to invite them all to punch and cookies upstairs. Everyone gathers to make the climb. As Colby and Ann Lee come to the top of the stairs, they see I. frantically poking holes in the tops of enormous fruit juice cans.

"Martha always attends to this," I. says, giving a can to Colby. The paper cups are very small, and the first one Colby fills tips over and floods the card table, which I. has covered with a poinsettia-printed paper cloth.

Several people come forward with napkins.

I. brings the next cup to Eloise, and as he watches his friend, Colby realizes that he reveres this woman, that her ridiculousness is, for I., a proof of grace.

Colby then introduces Ann Lee to I., stumbling over both their names. "Introduce yourselves!" he says at last, trying to make a joke of it.

"What does the I. stand for?" she asks.

"Isaiah. When I was little, I used to be teased."

They look at each other, shake hands, continue to look at each other. Neither of them is particularly graceful; their curiosity reigns. Colby circles them, embarrassed, finally brings his arm down through the air between them: "Enough!"

"Colby's been my friend since he came here," I. says, to cover his retreat. "It's only a year but it seems longer!"

Colby coughs and laughs.

Ann Lee says, "I think I know what you mean." She packs a good deal into that — promises to be tolerant which Colby finds condescending.

"You sound as though you're going to have to restrain yourself from doing me harm," he complains. "You're only going to be here a few weeks, how are you going to harm anybody?"

I. and Ann Lee laugh, and then I. says, "It's the short stops that do it. Before we were married, Martha came to visit me once for two days. I was in pieces."

Ann Lee says, "Why are you so afraid of Col getting hurt?"

I. considers. "Because he's gone along without hurting anybody for so long, he's lost the habit of self-defense. . . . You see this man here" — Colby is writhing — "he seems to be good-looking —"

"I've seen worse," Ann Lee says with a radiant smile.

"A talented teacher, and then we have to put up with the fact that his life is designed to spare him pain. Just that. He's the straight man to his own Fate."

Eloise Longham appears at I.'s side. "Whose pain?" she inquires.

I. introduces Colby and explains that it is his pain.

Eloise laughs. "I've spent my life making use of it. Is this where you ordinarily have your readings?"

I. says, "The reason there are so few is that this university is big on urban studies."

"I'm not complaining," she says. "They seemed receptive. Of course I'm used to a different kind of audience, more restless, noisier, more versed. But these" — she lowers her voice — "these have such sweetness, sheep in a field . . ."

"We're starved here for poetry," I. says. "We live in the middle of highways."

"I read all over the Midwest," Eloise tells them, hooking a finger in her blue bead necklace. "I like the readings. We don't shock each other in any acknowledged way."

Ann Lee introduces herself; Colby thinks her head-duck is an emblem for a curtsy. She immediately asks Eloise where she is staying.

"I've found a nice room — I. helped me. A Mrs. Faversham."

I. explains, "South Third, a widow fallen on hard times. She rents out a bedroom, makes breakfast."

"Unfortunately not served in bed," Eloise remarks. "I'll have to wait for that till I get back to the Chelsea Hotel."

"The Chelsea Hotel is a fleabag!" Ann Lee is surprised out of her usual tact. Quickly, she asks, "How much does this lady charge?"

"Are you looking for a place to stay?" I. asks.

"The Mayflower'll eat up everything I make."

Colby says, "I wanted to talk to you about this. I've already spoken to Martha."

"It's arranged," I. says.

Ann Lee asks if he means it and I. says he does. They begin to talk about her services.

"New baby?" Eloise asks when she hears about the routine.

"I told you," I. says. "My wife. My wife and me. We had a little girl."

Eloise says, "I remember . . . I have to get an early start in the morning for that place in Tennessee . . . Bethel? Halfway between Memphis and somewhere else. My daughter is staying there with a weaver. She's twenty-one, she went over to her father when we were divorced."

Ann Lee says, "She must be looking forward to seeing you."

Eloise stares at her. "Do you think so? I always thought there was something about me that drove her off."

"Don't believe that," Ann Lee says.

She is fitting in so smoothly that Colby feels obliged to take her by the elbow, remind her of his presence.

Now the Indian comes up to tell Eloise that he is alone in the world and that her poems have made him feel for a moment less alone. Colby, watching Eloise drink in the words, feels a pain he does not want to tolerate for the loneliness of the world.

"Let's go," he tells Ann Lee.

She is talking to I., she will not leave, and Colby stands first on one foot and then on the other.

At last he gets her to the door; she gets her coat on (she has borrowed a beautiful tweed from Grant Tom's stylish wife) and neatly ties herself up with the coat's long sash. "There." She looks at him. "Colby, you know I am going to have to disappoint you."

He wants to sink down on the floor and bury his face in her knees, plead with her like a starving man, like one of the pathetic remnant who listened to the reading. Instead he stands mute, accepting her judgment, and then drives her back to the Mayflower, chatting about poetry.

He walks her into the lobby and watches her start up the stairs they went up together only the day before. Back in his car, he puts his head down on the steering wheel.

8

"GRANT TOM SAYS you can come *this time*," Ann Lee says, with emphasis, when Colby calls her at the theater the next morning. He has left his class and he is sweating, faint with his own ridiculousness; he has rushed down the hall with a dime between his fingers, repeating the theater's telephone number, just to get to her, reach her, speak to her, at least. She says he can come to rehearsal.

"What time?"

"Be here at two o'clock. I'll meet you at the door."

She sounds neither pleased nor displeased but neutral, a woman with a certain something to give. Colby is chilled by her statement that he can only be received this time, that he cannot be welcomed regularly in the theater, that he must make do, or fill up the time with something else.

After he has hung up, he remembers his Victorian novels seminar at two and tries to call her back, but the phone in the theater is not answered. He calls one of his graduate students and asks him to take over the seminar. The boy is so flattered that Colby is ashamed.

Rushing back to his class, which he left in full swing,

Colby remembers that he never called himself a teacher. He fell into this life because of his wife and her father. He remembers talking to his father-in-law, ten years before, in the smoky study above a busy street in Cambridge.

"I don't have the calling," Colby said to quell his father-in-law's complaints. He wanted to twiddle his thumbs like a madman and, to prevent that, he stuffed his hands in his pockets. Laura apparently was complaining about his lack of zip, which corresponded — and he was horribly afraid his father-in-law might guess this — to his slackness, in bed.

"Aren't you working on a book?" his father-in-law asked him.

"No. The truth is, I don't have a decent idea. Why add to the sludge? It's all been said."

"That's beside the point."

Later that year, they went together to the Modern Language Association meeting in New York and for the first time had a few drinks together, buffeted by the enormous crowd. Laura was at home in bed in Cambridge, sick with winter flu and discontent, while her two men were on the wing; Colby thought it was the first time he had ever seen his father-in-law smile.

"You two getting along?" he asked.

"Well, Laura's sick a lot, I don't know if I'm to blame."

"Always was delicate, like her mother, she needs a baby to buck her up," the professor said.

"I'm just a mountain boy, I don't know anything about these things."

"It's time to start knowing. You've been married ten years."

"Nearly eleven."

"What do you have against children?"

"Nothing. Your daughter's teaching full-time, she won't even discuss it."

"It's not a question" — the eyeteeth signaled — "of discussion."

Colby felt the hateful connection, the prurient use of his life as a tool.

"I'm just a mountain boy," he repeated, an old joke among the three of them for when Colby couldn't figure the tip or failed to find a parking place or forgot to send Christmas cards to his colleagues.

As the class ends, Andrea Wesker approaches him to say, "You are still distracted!" She says it with an air of triumph.

Then she hands him a paper which is written in green ink on blue paper in a hand so complicated the composition looks like a wallpaper sample.

"What's this?"

"I hate the way typing looks, so machine made. Besides, it's winter, nearly; I wanted to do it spring."

"I can't read this." He tries to hand it back, but she folds her hands behind her back.

"My writing's very clear," she says.

Sighing, he places the paper in his briefcase and catches her smile of benediction.

Oh, Andrea, he thinks, if you knew: that plate of ribs, a month ago, was the height, the summit of our possibilities. He remembers the poet saying, "Neither a lover nor a father," and wonders if any other teacher has found that to be a profound though sorrowful relief.

He watches Andrea sway away. She does not even give him images; her calculation seems to wither her physical details. Yet masturbating, unillustrated, is a barren effort. In the end, he thinks, she is only another demand, an intolerable last straw, pleasure lost entirely in responsibility — that lethal asexual noun. He does not relish his morality. He tries to remember whether sex was playing, once. Was writing playing, once? Was there a sense of fun in words and deeds?

Andrea is gone with a last hopeful dart over her shoulder.

Colby, besieged, thinks that he is keeping her from something worse, that she will come out with an advanced degree because he has protected her from the fire-breathing boy in the next seat who would consume her with lust and demands. He lectures himself that it happens all the time: the bright girls — and only the girls are certifiably "bright," the boys may have a long-term promise but never that virgin gleam — are punched full of holes, semester after semester, by the boys who sleep with them. Silenced, distracted, booby-trapped by their sexuality, they stop turning in papers, sit in class bathed in unholy distraction. Punched full of holes, he repeats to himself, like the tin cans country boys used to stick on trees and shoot. Every one as honorable as a crow.

He knows that he is badly down, "separated from the experience of his generation" — for the experience of his generation, he knows, is not war or education but masturbating and endless impulsive fucking. He goes to the telephone in the hall to call Martha.

She is a long time answering. He lets it ring fifteen or twenty times, the receiver hooked between his shoulder and his ear, because he knows she is there — she is always there:

she left the hospital after her first twenty-four hours because she "needed to get home."

"Who is it?" she asks, breathless, and then, "I was nursing the baby, Col."

"I need to see you. I feel terrible."

A pause. "Col, this isn't a good time; the baby's cranky, I have to get her started on the other breast."

"I'll come in five minutes," he says.

She cannot refuse him; it is not in Martha's nature to refuse. He drives out Broadway, his right hand on the steering wheel and his left lying lightly between his legs.

She has told him that the front door is unlocked, and he steals in, waiting in the sloppy little foyer, where I.'s rubber boots are standing like household totems next to the hall tree. Martha calls, from the kitchen, "I'm in here."

He walks fast through the living room, where the herd of furniture is now peacefully drowsing, its mistress returned, and into the kitchen, where Martha is sitting in a chair next to the pine table. Her back is turned to him. A hunch of her shoulder tells him not to come around. He stands behind her, seeing something so familiar in the line of her neck, shoulder and crooked left arm that he begins to wonder if his mother had another baby, whether he once saw her nursing a ghost sibling when he thought he was the only one.

"Sit down," Martha says, using her free hand to gesture him to a chair.

He sits close behind her and studies the curls of hair on her neck as though he is memorizing a formula.

"What's wrong?" she asks, after an interval.

Colby is listening to the sucking. He can see the top of the baby's dark head over the crest of Martha's shoulder.

"How can I talk when you —"

"Well, then — don't!"

"I meant that as a joke. You remind me of things that never happened, make me feel I saw my own mother 'otherwise engaged.'"

"Don't worry, you're an only child, Col — you have all the earmarks."

"Yes, I know. I guess it's just Ann Lee. . . . She says this is serious."

"Oh, God. Her traveling days are over."

"No. I mean she says I'm serious and that changes everything."

Martha is suddenly listening with a degree of intensity.

"I think she may be right," Colby says.

"I know she's right. That's what you get for staying out of the world so long. You mean, she's trying to protect you?"

"I guess that's it."

"Well, I'll be glad when she moves in here. I like her sound."

"Did I. talk to you?"

"She did. She said she needed a place. She called me up. At that point, I didn't see how I could handle another walking need, but you make it sound as though she'll contribute."

"She knows a lot about babies, and she likes to share."

"I know a lot about babies: I've learned it all in one day. I'd like to have another woman around."

"I'll tell her. She'd probably like to move in right away."

"OK. So your troubles are over. But you know you can't sleep with her here."

"That's over, anyway."

"Then it is serious."

He looks at the groove in the back of her neck. "It's strange. Usually, I'm so glad not to have to take on the responsibility —"

"Responsibility?"

"You're not a man, Martha, though you're the most imaginative woman in the world."

"Well, then — be glad!" she says crisply.

He is glad because now he has something to carry to Ann Lee, something that satisfies his craving to give her a bunch of flowers.

A few minutes later, he hops into his car and spins down Grinstead Drive, both hands lightly on the wheel, this time, as though he has nothing to protect. It is a high clear day, warm as spring, and he tunes his radio to the all-rock station and rolls down his window an inch. It seems to him that things have taken a turn for the better, for unknown reasons; he is losing all his seriousness, he even laughs at the dj's joke.

He plunges into a parking lot a block from the mall and dances down the avenue, free as air and twice as light.

All because he has found Ann Lee a place.

Inside the Ten-Cent Theater, there is an atmosphere of hush. Colby stands for a while in the hall, trying to sort her voice out of the silence. At last he hears what he thinks is her chirp and starts off for the far left-hand corner. He enters in the middle of her sentence. She is standing on a raised platform with a man on either side and she is saying, "To start over!"

Grant Tom and two or three others are sitting on folding chairs, watching her.

"Try walking over to the bed," Grant Tom says.

She walks over to the bed, a makeshift affair, and sits herself on it. Colby is seeing her in a skirt for the first time, and her legs look too long. At that point, the man on her right goes off. She is left facing her left-hand man, who is tall and thin. He advances towards her, script in hand.

"Too close," Grant Tom calls, "you're not that far along yet," and Colby likes him again.

Ann Lee is concentrating on the actor; she lays her script down on the bed.

"All right, lie down," Grant Tom says.

"I don't think she would, at this point."

"Look, you're tired, you've been all night on the bus —"

"Yeah, but there's a man in the picture."

"Well, just lean back on your elbows, then."

"Worse!"

"Try it!"

She leans back on her elbows, and the pose is impossibly seductive. Her nipples show through her shirt. Colby wants to hide them with his hands.

"See what I mean?" she asks, sitting up. "You want me to be self-respecting, don't you?"

"I certainly do," Grant Tom says, "but we have to give him some encouragement."

"He's supposed to be an animal, he doesn't need encouragement, this is a rape, remember?"

Colby leans forward.

She has told him almost nothing about her role except that it is the female lead, and Colby assumed, since the Ten-Cent generally does modest little two-bit comedies with a

British flavor, that it was another one of these, a mild four-character laugh. Now he is watching Ann Lee lying back on the stage bed.

The thin-faced actor advances and Ann Lee cringes. Colby never expected in this life to see her cringe. Her knees seem to fold in the wrong way, and she reaches behind her to feel for the wall. The wall is further away, and her hand slides down through the air. Then the man is on top of her. Colby can see the soles of his shoes.

"That's more like it," Grant Tom says.

Ann Lee is turning her face from side to side to escape the man's lips. Colby wonders if she hates his breath. He looks like the kind of man who would have bad breath, made worse by a pine mouth lotion.

This is just a play, Colby repeats to himself.

The man is flat on top of her now. Colby can see Ann Lee's bare knee turned out, and he stands up. He is hot, he snatches at his collar, loosens his top button, he is burning.

The man begins to hump her. Colby can see the motions. Ann Lee is fighting with her hands and kicking with her feet and he hears her say, breathlessly, "Is this the way you like it? Raping? Is this the way?"

Colby stumbles up to Grant Tom. "This is no good," he says in a thick voice.

Grant Tom jerks around, startled. Then he recognizes Colby and pats a seat, next to him. "Sit down, friend." But Colby stands, weaving like a drunkard, still jerking at his collar.

"You're here too much, you know," Grant Tom says kindly. Then he calls to the stage, "Take five!"

The action stops; Colby can feel it stop even before he turns to check.

"You can't do this to her," he says, thick-tongued, stupefied by his own indignation.

"It's a tough play," Grant Tom says, gauging Colby. "You're new to the theater, aren't you?"

"Listen, I lived in Boston, New York, we used to go to all the plays. . . . It's not her kind of part!"

"She's a good actress, she can make it her kind of part."

Ann Lee is standing beside him now. She is standing absolutely still. "Colby, don't come in here and make trouble," she says.

"I don't want to see you fucked on the stage."

"Look, this is acting — you ought to know the difference."

"That guy with his hips —!"

Grant Tom stops them both with a flap of his hand. "This is a strong play. This is a strong role. Ann Lee has that, that strength. It's good for people to see that."

Colby turns on his heel. He want to efface them, destroy them both, because he knows if they continue to oppose him, he will burst into tears.

"Her dignity," he says through clamped teeth and then can't say any more.

Grant Tom puts his hand on Colby's shoulder. "I know how you feel. My wife used to act. I had to make her stop it, after a while. But you two aren't married."

Colby looks at him with gratitude.

"Yeah, we're not married, Mister," Ann Lee says in the coarsest accent Colby has heard her use.

"He cares about you," Grant Tom says.

A smaller person is coming with paper cups of coffee; Colby accepts one but does not drink.

Ann Lee's voice is still harsh. "I love this part, Col. It's about a woman who's had nothing but bad luck, spent her life in prison, now she's out; she has a chance to start over, but all these men are trying to get in her way."

"Get in her way?" Colby asks.

"Yeah, I mean literally . . ."

"Maybe I'm coming on too strong," the thin-faced actor suggests, behind them.

"No, that's the way I want it," Ann Lee says.

Colby begs Grant Tom, "Leave something to our imagination!"

Grant Tom seems to consider, but Colby knows he already has him on his side; he wants to keep him on his side, not alienate him with excessive demands, so he smiles. "Don't do anything just for me!"

Grant Tom smiles back, startled by the suggestion. Then he turns to the actor. "I think you might try just kind of kneeling over her, not getting right down on her — you know what I mean."

"What about those hip motions?" Colby asks.

Ann Lee demands, "Is he supposed to be raping me, or not?"

Other people have gathered; a girl with a dress over her arm, a boy carrying lightbulbs.

"I mean," Ann Lee says, "if he is not actually raping me, you make me out to be some kind of fool when I say that's what he's doing."

Grant Tom says, "I think you can afford to be more symbolic."

The actor nods. He seems relieved.

"Maybe she shouldn't hike her dress up so high," the girl with the dress over her arm puts in. "You can see she has on panty hose."

"Get her a garter belt and stockings."

"A mountain woman in a garter belt? White cotton underpants, the big kind."

Grant Tom says, for Colby, "I think it was Arnold's motions that were upsetting."

"Yes, that was the worst," Colby says. He cannot in spite of reason bear that his motions were the same as the motions of all the other men who have fucked her, and he knows now that there have been many, so many she couldn't possibly have kept count, and that all of them (except for the imaginative ones) started out by getting down on their hands and knees.

He wants her to be pure. It is wild. He wants her to be pure.

"I blame this play for this," he gasps, unsure whether he means the fact or the revelation.

"For what?" Grant Tom says, looking at Colby.

"For what's happening to her," Colby says.

At that moment, a young pale-faced woman with a notepad in her hand comes close to Colby and says, "You see, she's been raped all her life, in a way, that's all it's saying, it's just meant to show the kind of life she's had."

He looks at this delicate face, broad at the forehead, tapering to a narrow mouth and jaw.

"I'm Ellen Johnson. It's my play. I think I know what's bothering you," she says.

"She shouldn't be subjected to this."

Ann Lee laughs and says, "I'll skin you, Colby."

"It's meant to show," the pale playwright says, "what's happened to her, what happens to all women in this society if they don't conform. Of course it's not meant to be an actual rape. I think we've gone off the track."

"It can be done tastefully," Grant Tom says.

The boy with the lightbulbs shakes his head and passes on.

"I doubt that," Colby says. "Anyway, it's not taste we're talking about."

"It shouldn't actually be a rape," the playwright says.

Ann Lee asks, "What's the matter with you people? Are you afraid of the written word?" She whips the script out and slants a page at the light, drawing a line under a line with her fingernail. "'Ned falls on Elizabeth.' Is that meant to be symbolic?"

"I'd like to try it that way," the playwright says.

"We have to remember our audience," Grant Tom adds, slowly shifting gears; Colby can hear the internal grind. "I thought at first it was a good idea to show them something graphic, but now what Ellen says makes more sense. Let's run through it again, you kids ready? Arnold, this time just kneel on the edge of the bed, don't straddle it; let's see how it looks if we play it for the meaning."

Ann Lee, shaking herself like an annoyed hen, is coaxed back up onto the stage. Colby, exhausted, sinks into a chair next to the director.

They go through the scene again, the actor kneeling beside Ann Lee as though she is a sacrament.

Ellen, writing herself a note, looks up at Colby and smiles. "It does seem to work better this way."

"Yes," Colby says, and begins to wonder whether his life is going to change; whether suddenly things are going to begin to go right. He is not prepared for that.

He has also not reckoned on Ann Lee.

At the end of the scene, she beckons to him, and they go to stand at the entrance to a cubicle. The young costume designer passes and pins a lace collar against Ann Lee's sweater, steps back to admire the effect, then unpins it and goes on. All this time, Ann Lee is talking.

". . . no business coming here to mess things up. And you know it! No hold on me at all. No say in these things. No business . . ."

He reaches out to touch her, but she jerks her hand away.

"Just because one time . . . Doesn't give you the right . . ."

"It's not rights, it's feelings," he interrupts.

Now Grant Tom has come to help. "Calm down, Ann Lee. Honey, let's go get a cup of coffee."

She is raging and will not be stopped.

"It's all right," Colby says to Grant Tom, after a while. "I did interfere."

"Interfere!" And she is off again, blazing and snapping, flaring like a match flame in a crumpled nest of paper, everything going up in smoke and suddenly dying down.

She looks at Colby. "I'm sorry. It's just I don't like men sticking up for me, it's all wrong."

"What can I do for you, then?"

Grant Tom drops discreetly away.

"OK, if you want to do something for me, don't come here messing in my business . . ." He thinks she is off again, but she is not. "Just get your ass out of here. If you want to be useful, find me someplace to stay."

"I've already done that."

"Is that really going to work?"

"Martha's home with the baby, she needs your help. I talked to her about it. They have an extra room."

Then he sees an extraordinary thing. He sees this woman turn to him and smile. She reaches out and places her hands on his shoulders, and Colby, still encumbered by the past, remembers his mother putting her hands on his shoulders when she was pleased with him; then the memory passes and he feels each of Ann Lee's fingers and her stubby thumbs.

"Thank you," she says.

9

"YOU WHISK ALONG," Ann Lee says when Colby is driving her to the Weeklys.

"I'm in a hurry to get there. I. stays up half the night, but these days, Martha goes to bed early."

"I mean, you don't see anything."

"What is there to see in the dark, in this town?"

"At least you could smell," she says, rolling down her window and sticking her nose out. "I can smell the river, mud and catfish."

"Roll up the window, it's cold. I'll take you on a tour, tomorrow. We'll see the ducks in the graveyard and the museum and the old part of town they're trying to save, all those houses people moved out of forty years ago which have been rooming houses ever since. Sometimes it seems to me the past our parents spent their lives trying to escape is being tied up in paper and ribbons in this town."

"Prettified."

"Yes."

"Sort of like outdoor plumbing."

"They even have a book out on alleys."

It is fun to sing this duet.

He goes on, "When I think what alleys meant to my mother . . . We had a kind of an alley behind the house, at least there were a few shacks on it, and it was full of things that interest kids — old boxes, heaps of used furniture, some kind of stranded car — and she was always saying to me, 'Stay out of that alley. Don't be an alley cat.' Her dream was to get out of town, buy a house in the one high-class subdivision. It was called Angora Heights."

Ann Lee laughs ambiguously. They are passing through the Highlands, where, Colby explains, there are no hills. Along the road, the Tudor houses sit cheek by jowl. "Is this where they live?" Ann Lee asks.

"A little further on." He wants to tell her that Willow Street is nicer, that the room the Weeklys will give her looks out into a nest of a magnolia tree; but he is embarrassed by his own enthusiasm. He grips the steering wheel.

Yet she has made no criticism, has never said that he is taking her over, and as he edges his eyes towards her, he sees her hiking boots placed on the floorboard and thinks she might have grown up under his protection: that is the way she is acting, a galling comfort.

"Tell me more about you," he says.

"What do you want to hear about?"

"Your family . . ."

"I'm a middle child," she says, "the oldest girl. I had to take care of the others."

"Your father —"

"Out of work most of his life, I told you: a coal miner with the black lung; we lived on disability." She is clipped;

then she relents. "My mother used to say he was the best dancer in Harlan County, and I do remember him taking me up against his shoulder when I was a tiny girl, taking me up against his shoulder and dancing me to the radio. Just that once. Most of the time he was drinking and lying around the house like deadwood."

"Well, it didn't hurt you," he says. She is kind and passes over that, and Colby wonders if she knows that he cannot bear to see the signs of suffering which, in his case, have left him feeling simple and strange. He longs to reach out and hold her, comfort her for the past and so blot it out, but he knows better than to try: the past is one of the parts he cannot reach.

"Here we are," he says, livening his voice. He turns into the tiny drive. Martha's kitchen window is lighted; the rest of the house is dark. He is glad it is night so Ann Lee can't see the chipped yellow paint and the ruff of scraggly bushes around the screen porch.

He stops the car, jumps out and opens her door.

She gets out quietly, glancing up at the big glossy magnolia, lit by the light from the kitchen widow. She steps up onto the porch and puts her hand out to start the glider. "We had one of these on the front porch. I was the only one ever sat in it. My aunt crocheted a pillow for it once, but Mama was afraid it would get spoiled in the rain."

"Rain?"

"Well, you know — the damp."

He takes her to the front door and opens it.

Inside, in the yellow pine front hall (Martha stripped off layers of paint to reveal these boards), Colby stops and looks up the stairs, smelling the dried weeds in the brown pot, the half-burned logs from the fire I. tried to start the first cold night, the chicken Martha fried for supper, interrupted by a sweet smell, which is new. He lifts his nose, sniffing.

"You smell the baby," Ann Lee says. "Most men never do like a baby in the house."

Martha hurries out of the kitchen, wiping floury hands across the dish towel she has tucked in her waist.

"Here you are," she says, holding up her palms as though to reflect Ann Lee's face.

Ann Lee stands quietly, submitting to the introduction, the quick embarrassed survey, and then Martha, determined, kisses her cheek.

"It's not much of a room," Martha begins to explain. "Col said you needed a place to stay but I can't guarantee it'll be as comfortable as the Mayflower."

"I sleep on floors, I've slept in barns," Ann Lee says as though it is the beginning of a chant. "The Mayflower is too expensive for me." Then she gives Martha a short bright look. "You are very kind to take me in, a perfect stranger. I'll help you any way I can, any way you'll let me. Will you let me help with your baby?"

Martha hesitates; they are already at the nub. "You know, it's the strangest thing — I'm ashamed to admit it — but at this point, I can't bear for anybody to touch her. I don't even want her own father to touch her."

Ann Lee nods. "You must be nursing her."

"Yes — you think that's it? She's so necessary to me, I mean in a purely physical way. I couldn't get through the day without her, and I always thought it would be the other way around — she wouldn't be able to get through the day without me. But she can always take a bottle — not that I've tried, yet."

"We'll get her started on that," Ann Lee says, taking off her jacket and handing it to Colby. "My mother only nursed one of hers, the youngest, and he was always the one she couldn't bear to let go of; the rest of us she farmed out to her sisters and things, but little Jimmy was her lap baby. We don't want that to happen to you."

"Oh no?"

Ann Lee is openly gauging Martha now, and Colby shifts, feeling outside of things, then goes to the closet to hang up their jackets.

"I don't believe you'll go on wanting to be that close," Ann Lee says mildly.

Colby asks, "If you won't let her touch the baby, what is she going to do?"

Ann Lee answers for Martha. "I can always cook, I can clean up, do errands, wash the baby's diapers."

Martha asks, "You'd be willing?"

"I'm not a guest here, after all. I want to work for my keep."

"You'll be one of the family," Martha says.

"I never got to be that," Colby exclaims. He is delighted when the two women smile.

Ann Lee reaches out and touches his shoulder. "We'll let you be a regular visitor," she says.

"Where's I.?" Colby asks, wanting to complete the circle.

Martha explains to Ann Lee, "My husband is upstairs working. I try to keep him from being interrupted too often.

He has this horde of students, they come to him for everything — personal problems, the whole thing."

Ann Lee nods. "I want to see him."

"Have you got your luggage?"

"Just this knapsack. I travel light!"

"That's the only way," Martha says, and Colby realizes that she is already committed to liking everything about Ann Lee. "Do you want to see your room?"

"Yes."

There is no doubting her interest.

Martha starts up the stairs, whose banister she has stripped to a pale banana color; the spindles are knock-kneed, bulbous, half-stripped: they keep red stockings of paint.

Colby, following Ann Lee, wants to put his two hands on her neat rear end. He is not certain anymore how she would react, and he touches, at that, the edge of his pain.

They cross the hall, and Martha knocks softly at I.'s study door; through the crack, Colby sees him leaning back in his desk chair, abstracted, staring at a corner of the ceiling. He jumps up and comes out as though relieved of his abstraction. Taking hold of Ann Lee's hands, he gazes at her with his mild billy-goat eyes, his eyebrows bristling like feelers; then he retreats back into his study, shooed by Martha, who says she is sure he has something better to do, and the procession rounds the corner to the baby's room.

They lean over the crib, where it is sleeping, folded. Colby sees the features have not yet risen; the forehead remains out of proportion, a long slope. The lips are gathered towards the bunched hand. "Has she found her thumb yet?" Ann Lee asks in a normal voice, and both Martha and Colby hush her. "Not yet," Martha whispers; the baby is stirring, a faint frown passes over the forehead, then it settles itself again on its stomach, hunching into the mattress. Colby sniffs the sweet smell, struggles for words, finds none, turns to leave. The two women follow him, smiling.

They pass on to the spare room. Martha flips on the ceiling light. Colby sees a narrow bed with a corduroy spread, a shelf of books, a fireplace with a coal grate and polished fender. Martha's collection of bisque dolls is arranged on the mantel: one in a cane chair, one standing, another with its back turned to show the ridges which stand on its skull for hair.

Ann Lee asks, "Are those yours?"

Martha begins to explain why and when she collected them.

Ann Lee interrupts her, "Would you mind — I don't like them much. Could they go someplace else?"

Even Martha is stalled and about to be affronted when Colby asks, "What is it about them, Ann Lee?"

She turns to him, troubled. "They remind me of something bad in my life: dolltime. I'd rather not share a room with them."

He is so eager to know.

Martha, recovering, says, "Of course I'll take them away," and sweeps the whole collection into the crook of her arm.

As she goes out to put the dolls away, Colby asks Ann Lee, "What is it?"

He has to wonder as she turns again whether this first evidence of pain is, for him, useful only as a door, a way to get to her.

"They remind me of a child," she says. "That seems funny but it's true. A child I lost."

"Lost?"

"An abortion — the usual thing. Five years ago next March. I was ten weeks along, I couldn't make up my mind."

Colby hears Martha coming back and asks, "Will you tell me about it, some other time?"

"Colby, you wouldn't want to know."

"I want to know," he says, sure that this is a chance he can't afford to miss.

"I'll think about it."

"Come and have some herb tea," Martha says, sheepish as though she has interrupted them making love, and they follow her downstairs.

In the kitchen, Ann Lee begins to tidy up. She takes the plates out of the drainer and puts them away, finding their places easily, as though there is a universal code. Martha sets the kettle on the flame and gets out the cups.

Colby, hearing their talk, thinks that he will never be able to find a place between them. They have their whole shared female life as common ground. He wonders why he has never found this shared ground with a man; even with I., it is the specifics — their teaching, the books they've read, their shared expeditions — not this magical melting into common experience.

He goes upstairs to sit with I., who is laboring on a poem. He wants to tell his friend that he is hopelessly jealous of every aspect of Ann Lee which does not belong, or potentially belong, to him. He does not want to shock I., however, who would accept sexual descriptions but would be honestly offended by other signs of passionate attempted ownership, would possibly connect them to the lust for possessions which drives him from supermarkets and department stores. Colby can already hear him exclaim, "You are turning this woman into a thing!" He wonders if Martha ever wishes that I. would turn her into a thing instead of keeping her so scrupulously unpossessed, knows this is mean-spirited and asks I. to read out loud the stanza he has just completed.

It is about the early days in Kentucky, the fear of Indian attack.

Colby goes down after a while to say good night to Ann Lee. He tries not to notice how close together the two women are sitting, huddled over their cups of Lemon Mist.

He tells Ann Lee he will come in the morning and take her sightseeing, before her rehearsal, then leaves triumphant: she is far from the bus line and will have to depend on him for transportation.

As he lets himself out, he hears the baby begin to howl.

10

COLBY WAKES UP EARLY the next morning. He is in his nest. The covers of the bed smell of several weeks' sleep; the worn green wool blanket smells of camp; the pillow, under the pillowcase, crackles with wads of some anonymous fiber and seems to smell, in spite of everything Colby can marshal to argue against the possibility, of his mother.

It is warm. It is nearly dark. After his years in the East, Colby resents the western, early-morning darkness. It makes it even harder to get up. Besides, his class is in the afternoon today, and he is not due to pick up Ann Lee until ten.

He burrows under the covers, drawing them over his head and relishing the memory of his mother twitching the sheet: "Colby, you'll suffocate." Even she, with her righteous inquisitiveness about every branch of his life, had not quite dared to pluck the covers back.

He puts his hand on his cock. In the last year, he has stopped masturbating except for a rare bout of self-pity, when he strokes himself as though to soothe a wound. Now he thinks he should begin again, as a duty, for Ann Lee's sake. Otherwise he may overwhelm her with the rages of his thwarted appetite. It is a nice thought. Colby does not imagine himself a sensual being. His marriage and the few brief affairs which preceded it were caused by other considerations — affection, boredom, momentary need. Sex has been only the offshoot of other, more dramatic interests. He knows this. He strokes his cock. Still, he is proud of his quick erection, which seems as it always has since boyhood, immense. At least he does not need to worry about his size.

Coming, he sees Ann Lee being whipped.

He jumps up, washes and begins to dress. The cool water shocks him, bringing a bout of self-reproach. All he has read does not prepare him to accept this, all his decent arguments in his own defense have a tin sound, like arguments he has heard in defense of prostitution, or slavery.

It is essential, now, to get to her. He knows when he looks at her, kisses her cheek, touches her hand his affection will rise and he will forget this.

He looks at himself in astonishment in the bathroom mirror. Then he begins to shave with great care, as though the razor might leap from his hand and cut his throat. I was a man who was married for eleven years to a frigid woman and never looked outside; I was a man who spent ten years single and only looked at women as impediments. He wonders about the source of these flashes, which have nothing to do with his personality, with his chosen life.

His father's laugh when he swiped Colby's mother, hard, on the rear end — how Colby hated that! The way his father laughed! And his mother, in the midst of her protest, smiled in a foolish way and wiped her hands on the back of her skirt as though to wipe off the marks. His father left marks —

Colby thinks he saw them, long, red weals on his mother's buttocks and thighs.

He rushes to his car. Turning on the radio, he listens to an old Noël Coward song: "The Rest of Your Life." Colby likes the song. The lyrics seem as ancient as the hieroglyphs on the pyramids. He does not think he has felt that promise — that self-confidence — that continuity. What has happened to the future of his tender feelings? They seem to live like puppies around his feet, nibbling and whining for food, for attention, with no hold on the future. All that is certain is that they will die. Even Ann Lee . . .

He tries to see her in some future scene, sitting on a chair, talking, or taking out the trash, but he cannot see it, he has no frame for Ann Lee. Instead he sees his ex-wife in a group of familiar poses: trying on a new dress, looking up from stirring something on the stove, waving off his kisses when she was sitting next to her high-intensity lamp correcting papers, crying in bed one Sunday morning while he sat helplessly watching her — "There's nothing to do today, there's nothing to do . . ." Laura has become, at last, her scenes, and he thinks he will be able to see her, if he ever sees her again, almost painlessly.

He is driving all this time, crashing into potholes. To calm himself, he looks at the graveyard wall; he will bring Ann Lee there later; it is one of the town's attractions. He wonders if he will be buried there, when his time comes, under a modest stone: "Colby Winn, English teacher." She will be beside him, her maiden name piously included. He tries to think of an epitaph which will serve them both and comes up with one he has seen on New England graves:

If this you see
Remember me.
As I am now
You soon must be.

A Southerner would never say that. He would have more decency.

The Weeklys' house, in the bright early-morning sun, looks shabby but anchored, a dory at a dock; Colby imagines he can see the frame walls rising and falling under the light pressure of the water. For the first time, he feels it is the right place for Ann Lee; it has enough motion in it.

He parks rakishly in the driveway — I.'s terrible old Pontiac is gone, he has a nine o'clock class — and jumps up onto the porch. He wishes the two women were at the window to admire his verve. Instead, he sees Martha's canary, and a low bench of many-branched plants.

He rings, then knocks. The house answers with its own peculiar blend of silence. There is no human sound, however. Colby tries the door. To his surprise, it is locked. He shivers and shifts his weight impatiently. He remembers standing like this once before, late at night, when he dropped in unexpectedly; finally I. and Martha came downstairs, sheepishly, adjusting various fasteners, and Colby laughed silently, knowing that he had almost interrupted the primal scene.

At last Martha comes slowly down the hall — he can see her through a clear patch on the stained glass window. She has the baby in her right arm, and she opens the door awkwardly with her left hand.

"Why didn't you come on in?" she asks. She is looking pale.

"It was locked," Colby says, hanging back.

"Ann Lee likes locking up. She was getting me started, we didn't hear the door."

She turns to lead him down the hall.

"Getting you started?"

"It's the nursing. I think I was anxious. She knows a lot about it from her mother."

"I didn't think you wanted her to touch the baby."

"This is me, not the baby," Martha says as though he is being obtuse.

In the kitchen, Ann Lee is sitting with her legs crossed at the ankle, looking as though she is honoring the old red chair.

"They never told her anything about nursing at the hospital," she says, turning up her cheek in a wifely way for Colby's kiss. Colby opens his mouth as though to suck in part of her cheek; he leaves a small damp mark, which she wipes off with the back of her hand.

"Anything . . . ?"

"Women have to be taught, it doesn't come naturally anymore. After all, the culture has practically exterminated nursing."

"Can you exterminate an instinct?"

She is not interested. In a businesslike way, she instructs Martha to return to her seat in the other red chair. The two women sit, knee to knee, the baby laid between them. She is beginning to crank and wave her fists, and Colby takes a look at her.

How could that be I.'s, he thinks. It's so fat! The baby even has red wrinkles on its neck.

It is also smelling very strong. I. sometimes smells of herb tea or of Ivory soap or of vitamin capsules (these last have a crushed, sharp smell), which he takes, in quantities, every day.

"Try the left side," Ann Lee says. She watches as Martha unbuttons her blouse and takes out a round hard breast, the nipple straining, dotted with milk.

Colby looks at a wall.

The baby begins to yammer — Colby has never heard such a soulless sound. It is a machine on the blink, a washer loaded wrong, pounding away on one sodden towel. My God how the thing can howl! He wonders if this has been going on all night.

"She's hungry," Ann Lee says proudly. "Now, remember, prop her against your upper arm — crook your arm, like this, and put your hand under her rear end. Now take your nipple between the first two fingers of your right hand —"

"Just like the Renaissance madonnas," Colby says, but nobody laughs.

"And just push it back against the roof of her mouth. There, she's rooting for it."

The baby is making fiendish squawks. Colby sees its square pink hands beating the air. Its mouth is pushed out, it wags and plunges its head, but the big firm nipple will not fit in, the baby keeps losing it; finally, she flings back her head and howls.

Martha shifts the baby around, trying to force her to get a purchase.

Ann Lee gets down on her knees in front of Martha. Placing the baby's head in position with her right hand, holding the head firmly, she seizes Martha's nipple between the first two fingers of her left hand and plunges it into the baby's mouth.

The baby rolls her head, widens her eyes, seems about to open her gums and expel the nipple. Ann Lee presses her finger above Martha's nipple, and Colby sees a drop of milk pool at the corner of the baby's mouth. A look of astonishment crosses the wrinkled face. Suddenly the gums clamp. The baby snorts and begins to suck.

Ann Lee lets go and claps her hands.

Then she stands up and looks down at her new friend. Martha has bowed her head to watch the baby, whose free hand keeps time in the air. Her eyes are beginning to close. She is sucking with regular, powerful contractions of her whole mouth and jaw. Her choking swallow is loud as the milk passes down. Some overflows her mouth and trickles down her chin. Ann Lee goes to the paper towel roll and brings back a bit, which she sticks under the baby's chin.

Then they all sit and stare.

Ann Lee turns to Colby finally. "Would you like something, a cup of tea?"

"Nothing right now."

11

LATER ON, Colby drives Ann Lee through the wrought-iron gates to the graveyard. He stops the car and directs her to admire the leaves and vines, the enormous hinges half-buried in the limestone posts.

"When you don't have much to look at, you have to look at what you do have," he explains. "These gates were designed by a Frenchman, I forget his name, made in a foundry in France and shipped over here. I used to think someday I'd see them closed. Now I'm just glad they're here at all — you have to rest your eyes!" He looks around at the barricade which surrounds the graveyard: hamburger stands, gasoline stations, and the peaked, sad roof of an old frame house.

They drive on. "Where are we going?" Ann Lee asks in a voice which is new to Colby. She must be tired.

"Well, we have an hour till your rehearsal."

"Yes," she says, as though not relishing the prospect.

"I've gotten to like this town — all its special places; I want to show them to you, show you the sights." He reaches over and touches the back of her hand.

Her hand feels cool and slack, boneless. He is worried about her. Something essential to her framework seems to have been left behind with Martha and the baby.

"Would you like to see the sights with me?" he asks sadly.

"Yes," she says, with her direct look, and he knows she is trying, with what energy she has left, to mend his disappointment.

"All right! I'll show you the best grave." They drive along slowly behind a funeral procession, finally passing it as the limousines, slow as whales, pull over to park beside a green tent and a mound covered with artificial grass.

"What was that angel?" Ann Lee asks.

"What? On top of the gate? I didn't think you noticed. That was Thorwaldsen's *Angel of the Resurrection.*"

"Do you believe in that?"

"What? The resurrection?" She nods. "I believe there are times in life like the resurrection."

"That's not very nice."

"It's nice! I'm not joking, Ann Lee. I don't believe in a resurrection after death because (and this may surprise you) I believe in the body. Now, I know that sounds ridiculous."

" 'The resurrection of the body, and the life everlasting . . .' "

"Is that what you believe?"

"No. The body's too bad for that."

"Stinking like that baby," he hazards.

"No, that was just shit. She was giving her vitamin drops!"

Colby doesn't want to hear any more about that. "This used to be called Cave Farm," he tells her quickly, remembering his first week here, before he met I., when he walked the city with a guidebook as though he was in Europe. There were only a few sights in the guidebook, each amply described. "It became a graveyard in the eighteen forties and grew rapidly, but somehow I still think of it as a farm, a good one, with a big harvest." He waves his arm at the rolling hills, the rows of gravestones, which curve like rows of corn. "I'll show you my favorite one, first, I always believe in starting with the dessert —"

He stops the car in front of a large monument on which two life-sized white marble women turn to face each other; dressed in long limp garments, crowned with flowers, they peer intently into each other's faces.

"What's that?" Ann Lee asks.

"Two sisters who married nobility. The one called Mary Elizabeth married a German baron who was killed when his yacht was rammed by the Kaiser's. The one called Gwuendaline married a marquis. The first one had a son and a castle in Germany. She died of a flu she caught at an open-air fete, and the little boy brought her body back here — by then he was grown. His grandfather was an actor's son who made good on real estate speculations here, after the Civil War. You see, life can be interesting, even in Louisville."

Ann Lee says, "They're pretty, in a way."

"Yes, in an enormous way. I climbed up on the base one time when I thought I was going to die of loneliness and be buried under a plain marker and I realized they are life-sized, a little shorter than me, but from down here, they look enormous."

He drives her on to the lake, where she is amazed by the numbers of geese and ducks, all preening or sleeping on one leg around the plucked edge of the water. They watch a mallard and his mate glide into the water, their green heads gleaming in the sun. It is as warm as May; Colby takes off his jacket.

"I'm as proud of this place as if I'd invented it," he says.

Then they go to look at the baby graves. There are a lot of them in the old part, scattered like teeth in front of the larger monuments. The smallness of the baby stones bothers Colby; he thinks of it as a kind of cheese paring. Also the inscriptions are short, and he has it in mind that that, too, was to save money. "Baby boy," he reads to Ann Lee, who is standing at a little distance, looking down. "May eleventh, eighteen-eighty-one to June one, eighteen-eighty-one. They didn't even have time to name it." Then he points out a recumbent lamb on top of one of the stones; smoothed by rain, it looks like a small ridged loaf.

Ann Lee is looking at the grave of a girl. "Little Sunbeam. You think that was really her name?" Before Colby can answer, she goes on, "I was pregnant, once. Five years ago."

Colby stands at her elbow in silence. He is unwilling to remind her that he knows.

"Yes. I couldn't make up my mind what to do: I was that foolish. I didn't even like the man, I didn't want to see him again, but I tried to find some way to hold on to that baby. That was what was ridiculous. I came down to Cincinnati finally to get rid of it. But it was too late. I'd waited too long."

Colby does not want to hear, but he cannot bear to stop her.

"They made a fuss," she says. "The doctors. Acted as though I was killing something. I wasn't killing something, they were. I was only ten weeks along. I couldn't get over it for the longest time, couldn't stop crying.

"You know," she goes on after a while, "there's only one way to make sure it won't happen again."

"Now, wait."

"No, all those devices fail, I know that. Every one of them lets you down."

"You can't live your life that way!"

"I can. I've taken enough risks already," she says.

"You took one risk with me!"

"That was safe. I told you. That was my safe time."

"Ann Lee, honey, there are ways —"

"Ways, and ways. I don't want anything to do with all that. Don't start to argue with me, you won't get anywhere, you'll just make me mad. You don't know anything about it all; men don't. You don't know what a woman goes through. Everything dies. Everything. I won't lay myself open to that again."

Avoiding her face, Colby looks down at his feet. A trickle of water runs down the cement path, blackening it. Grave water.

He says, "I don't want you to make up your mind like this. It's too soon."

"I made it up a long time ago. You were such a surprise. You made me feel as though those things didn't happen, you made me feel as though I'd imagined it — the things that happened to me. But they did happen, Col. And I made up my mind —"

"Give me another chance," he pleads, looking down the hill to the lake where the matched mallards are swimming.

"I can't do that, Col. I can't fool around with my life."

The air smells hot and dry, as though they are at the edge of a great autumn fire; Colby imagines he can hear the crackling and crashing of trees mowed down by flame. He tries to think that he is only smelling Rubbertown. Ann Lee is looking at him.

"I'm sorry to have to say this."

"It must be something I did," Colby mumbles.

"No," she says.

"You weren't . . . satisfied."

"I've never been satisfied in my life and don't intend to be. You don't know me well enough to understand that."

"Give me a chance," he pleads. He wants to sink down on his knees in the dry grass.

"It's not a question of chance, Col — believe me. If it was going to be anyone, it could have been you."

She is looking at him calmly. The moment of anguish, when she spoke of her lost child, is passed.

"Is it because it may not last?"

"That's got something to do with it. I'm not modern, I don't know how to do without my own future."

"It might last." Suddenly, he is wary. "Of course, I don't know . . ."

She laughs. "There you go!"

"Well, I mean, I couldn't make up my mind, this fast . . ."

He realizes, with rage, that he has lost this battle.

"But you want to make up my mind," she says, seriously.

He does not dare touch her, although he knows that only touch can help now.

She says sadly, "I expect I won't be seeing much more of you."

"Oh, Ann Lee —"

"Now, don't apologize."

"Nothing's changed, we'll still see each other."

"We'll see," she says. "It must be almost eleven. Will you drive me down to the theater?"

As they turn in their disciplined lockstep and start towards the car, Colby tries to identify his pain. It is a cold hole, an ache, where life no longer fits. He cannot remember ever having wanted anything except for this pain to go. Filled up with other sensations — even with more violent suffering; at least then the core, the deep hollow, would be filled. He has drawn himself in his mind many times, an outline figure, full of spaces. It is the spaces that hurt.

The world seems to have lost its color. At the edge of the graveyard, the red dogwoods look rusty, and the air smells parched. A fine haze of industrial matter fills the air. He is angrier than he can believe, angry first of all at himself for not seeing, anymore, the limestone posts and the wrought-iron gates.

For the first time, he helps her into the car.

"Now you really are angry," she says as he climbs in on the other side.

"Ann Lee, I haven't felt — I told you, I've been on my own for ten years, I wasn't prepared for this."

She does not answer.

He switches lanes rapidly, shooting down Broadway, driving the way Southerners don't drive, hooked over the steering wheel, his thumb on the horn. Let anyone get in my way! He whips past a faded blue school bus labeled ZION BAPTIST CHURCH, Negroes, on their way to some sociable, the Great Society never got to them — it passed him by, also. A woman in a pink turban stares down at him from the bus window. Let them get in my way, they'll see what a white man can do. He passes, honking.

"You are segregating me," he says, then realizes from the quality of Ann Lee's silence that she is not even going to argue with him about his ridiculous phrase. She is staring ahead, already in the theater, and he wishes he had the gall to stop and put her out, let her ride the ZION BAPTIST CHURCH.

Broadway leads into the center city, slumped in terminal decay. Between gasoline stations, narrow frame houses are set each at the top of three steps, which lead down to the sidewalk; these houses have turrets and little lawns. Some of them have been faced with display windows, full of half-dead plants and hopeful signs: Jerry Greider's Music School, all phases of the guitar, or Dressmaking, Alterations, quick and cheap. Behind these signs, people are waiting.

Further along, one of the houses has been pulled down to make way for a White Castle, and its neighbor has been leveled for a parking lot: VIOLATORS WILL BE TOWED AWAY. Am I a violator, he thinks, remembering how his mother used to lecture him about girls, their delicacy, how they needed his protection though he'd seen no signs of this, how he should be kind, until he wondered if she'd ever smelled

the girls in his class, as sour and sharp as boys if not worse. . . .
She, his mother, had an abbreviated view, and he wonders if
his father, in their calmer moments, ever tried to expand it
or was it all hopeless, hopeless, a wasted effort? . . .

GERTLES PLACE, BEER . . .

The warehouse for the department store looms up, next
to the railroad bridge lined with cattle cars. To the left, the
city stockyards, now scientifically run, no longer stink. The
cattle are tranquilized, clean, silent, herded to the slaughter-
house by cowboys on mopeds.

"When I see you again — when will I see you again? We
could go to Gertles Place, have some beer."

She does not answer.

"And you haven't seen the stockyards, they have a museum. All the instruments of execution from the poleax on.
They're talking about reenactments."

"Colby, can't we be —"

"Friends?"

"Not friends. It's too hot for that."

"Then what?"

"I don't know."

Past the jumble of a newsstand where on Sundays Colby
buys *The New York Times*.

"I used to go there every day, my first month here; when
I'd see the front page, that shade of black type, my heart
would start to pound. The big world still out there somewhere. The old man was so proud of getting the paper the
same day."

"Why did you move down here?"

"Scared I couldn't make it, up there. I'd seen all the signs."

"Look, you can take me out if you want, show me places."

"What places." He doesn't have the strength to make it a question.

"Places. Where you were born, your part of the state."

"Pineville?" He is amazed. "There's nothing there."

"Your father's there, isn't he?"

"Well, yes. We hardly speak — I mean, I send him a card at Christmas."

"I'd like to meet him," she says.

Annoyed, Colby tells her, "I long ago gave up thinking I'd get something by going there — what do you call it, a Relationship, make up for lost time. It's him that's got to make up for lost time."

"Maybe I can help you."

"Oh, stop it."

"Just maybe." She is trying to win him now with her smile.

"Look, he did things to my mother — she's dead; if she was alive and I saw he'd learned how to treat her, that might make a difference."

"What's the use of going on blaming him?"

"You sound like those handbooks. If we can't be lovers, at least let's not be helpmeets."

And he laughs, in spite of himself.

"OK," she says. "That's a deal. . . . There's the library," she adds, pleased to recognize one landmark. "I went in there yesterday and took out a card."

"What are you going to read?"

"Probably nothing, I won't have the time, I've got a lot of lines to learn. I like to belong to the library, though; that's the first thing I do when I get to a new place."

They are at the mouth of the mall. Colby lets her out near a concrete flower box and a bench donated by the Lions Club. An old black woman is sitting on the bench with a plastic shopping bag, filled to bursting, at her feet.

Colby leans across the seat to speak to Ann Lee, who is already out but has not closed the door.

"What time shall I come to take you back to the Weeklys'?"

"I don't know. Don't worry. I'll take the bus."

"You forget where you are. There is a bus, it runs twice a day. You could stand here for hours."

"Or sit." She is about to close the car door.

"Wait!"

"I'll hitch, if I get stuck."

"When am I going to see you, Ann Lee?"

"Call me tonight," she says. "They'll let me talk on the telephone at the Weeklys', won't they?"

He remembers then that she is a lost girl. She has probably had this kind of job before, with all kinds of restrictions.

"Of course they will," he says. "What do you think?"

"Well, in some places —"

"Not the Weeklys. When shall I call — eight? Nine?" He already knows this will be the focus of his evening.

"Better say nine; by then we'll have the baby fed."

He is struck by her use of the plural. "OK, nine."

She closes the door. The old woman is smiling and nodding as though satisfied with the way they have played their scene.

He cannot pull swiftly and smartly away. He sits at the curb and watches her go up the mall, walking fast, Martha's blue jacket open and spreading out behind her.

12

I. IS STANDING at the window of his office in the new humanities building, looking at a patch of dead grass. Sunlight passes through the panes and crosses his face, bleaching it; he looks as old and dried as a bone in the desert, Colby thinks, and shifts in his canvas chair. I.'s office is furnished like a beach house, with canvas, rattan and cane. It is supposed to look cheerfully informal, but after three years of I.'s emotional sessions with his students, the cane is frayed, the canvas chairs are caving in and the look is of a summer house that has survived a hurricane.

"Human need," I. says, and taps a nail on the window. "See that girl over there? That lovely, wild, vivid girl? She was in here yesterday for two hours, crying. I couldn't get her to tell me what the trouble was. Nothing academic, of course, it never is — she came to hand in a really inspired paper on Keats. No. It's the world they can't handle."

Colby does not stand up to see this inspiration for I.'s compassion. Colby himself was an applicant when he first arrived; confused by the department, he came to I. for a reading on the place. I. knew everyone and discussed them

all with the same light-fingered malice. He told Colby which
instructor had been advanced because of his willingness to
make omelets at faculty parties, which one was the favorite of the dean's wife, which one would never get ahead because of his bachelorhood. Colby's blood chilled, at that.
"It's not the way to be, here," I. said, matter-of-factly. "Not
that I'm urging you to rush into anything —" But there was
the question of sociability, of being ready to give the right
kind of parties, small dinners, a little wine with some good
French cheese; and Colby, alone, would never dream of trying.

I. turns away from the window. "What would you say to
a walk?"

From his side glance as they slip out, Colby understands
that I. is avoiding a supplicant and hopes that his friend is
learning, at last, to guard his resources.

They walk across dried mud between the new science
building and the new wing of the library. It is coffee-break
time and the workmen are sitting or standing beside their
machinery; Colby envies them their camaraderie as he and I.
walk by in difficult silence. I.'s eyes are bent on the ground,
he is walking with his shoulders humped, his arms swinging;
invisible weights are pressing him down.

"What's wrong, I.?" Colby asks when they reach the
walled garden which is all that is left of the Victorian man-
sion where the university began.

I. opens the crusted iron gate and goes in. There is no pro-
vision for keeping up the garden, and it is heavily used by
students, yet its original plan remains intact: inlaid brick
walks radiate out from a central basin, where a cupid with

broken arms perches on a tiny world. There was a fountain here, but its workings are long broken. Triangular beds of trampled yet vigorous ivy separate the brick paths; stone benches, supported on griffins, are garlanded with graffiti but still upright. In spring, I. says, there are snowdrops beneath the ivy.

I. drops down on a bench and raises his face to catch the sun. Colby stands over him, ashamed of his gluttonous curiosity.

"I should have stayed to talk to that boy," I. says, sighing.

"How do you get them to talk to you? Mine never do."

I. shrugs. "They just talk."

"All you have to do is stand still and people gather around you, wanting your advice, your attention — anything."

"Does it ever occur to you . . . Sometimes I could use a little attention, myself." I.'s voice is drowsy.

"I never know when —"

"Well, now is the time." He wets his lips, preparing to speak personally, which Colby has never seen him even tempted to do. "It's the baby."

Startled, Colby asks, "What?"

"I started to say, up all night, howling, but that's not the problem. That's not it. She — your girlfriend — she was up with her. I can't say it's the inconvenience, I never have minded inconvenience, it means nothing to me. No. It's Martha."

Colby sits down beside him.

"I've never seen her like this before," I. says. "Distracted. Totally distracted. I'm a selfish man," he adds, opening his eyes to stare at Colby. "I never have made any other claim. I need Martha's attention. I can't come here and do what I do unless I have her attention, at home. She knows that, we've always been that way — emotional refueling," he says, grimacing at the phrase. "We even used to joke about it. Of course I knew the baby would bring some changes, but when Martha was in the kitchen this morning, holding her in her arms, and I came in and saw the edge of her profile, looking down —"

"A creature possessed," Colby says, trying humor.

"She didn't even know I was in the room."

"Giver her time, I. It's all new, now."

"I don't think the newness matters. It's the power of the demands."

He is speaking softly, in a slowed voice.

"What can I do?" Colby asks.

"Stay close to me, it's a bad time."

Having gone that far, I. leaps off the bench. "Let's take the rest of the day off, we deserve it. I don't have another class till four."

"I'll have to get back by three," Colby says. "I have a class then —" nervous already that the whole day will fall before I.'s demands. "Where shall we go?"

I. looks at him, bright-faced and mischievous. "I have a great idea." He leads Colby at a lope to the old blue Pontiac, sitting beached and slightly lopsided in the faculty parking lot, the university sticker on the bumper the only clean thing about it.

"Looks like you're getting a flat," Colby says, inspecting.

"Oh, just losing a little air."

I. shrugs, bored and irritated by anything mechanical,

then climbs into the car. Colby gets in beside him, soberly considering his fate. He wants to be back in time for his conference, and he knows enough about I. to know there is no spare tire in the trunk and no jack.

"I've got to be back by three o'clock . . ."

"Listen, my friend, this is an adventure."

Colby is shamed out of any further doubts. They drive down Third Street to Spaghetti Junction, where the big new interstates thread and wind; the signs are magical, mysterious — St. Louis, Cincinnati, Lexington — as though the whole world with its cities waits on the other side of the junction. There are no local signposts here. I. with amazing skill threads the cloverleaf, races in front of a truck (even truck drivers in the South, Colby notices, are too well-bred to honk), dips down and off the expressway and rides along between its elephantine legs. The river runs alongside.

"Where are you taking me?" Colby asks.

"You'll see."

They are at the edge of the river. The cobblestones make the car thunder and lurch, the sky is cut out by the expressway overhead. Colby usually stays away from the river, which is large and ugly and threatening here above the locks, racing full tilt at all seasons, carrying along everything it finds loose. He looks at it apprehensively. Even now, in October, the river is ominously swollen and dark, livid with flashes of oily pink; it is carrying grease-blackened logs, parts of old crates, an inflated green plastic garbage bag riding along at a rakish angle.

They pass a hell of busted and burnt-out boxcars, left from some forgotten disaster, and the back half of an enormous truck, its roof peeled by an overpass. Further along, a crane with a broken neck extends its injury. This is a grave-yard for abused machinery and the neat packets of squashed cars. I. threads through it rapidly and stops at the edge of the burdened water. They step out onto cobblestones.

A rowboat and its man are waiting.

"Is this for us?" Colby asks.

"I want you to meet my friend, Captain Clayton," I. says, striding towards the man. Colby follows cautiously.

The man by the boat is black and small and hunched. He is wearing a stained pea jacket and a cap with woolly flaps, which are pulled down over his ears. He is also wearing a pair of enormous black rubber waders, over nothing, Colby suspects; he is tucking in his pea jacket as though to cover a gap.

I. puts his palm in the middle of the captain's back and propels him directly at Colby. Colby has no choice but to ex-tend his hand and allow it to be grasped and wrung by a powerful hand.

"Captain here is always agreeable to taking us over to the old Fountain Ferry," I. says. "River not too high, Captain?" I. speaks without condescension in a singsong voice, all the time gazing out at the oily water.

"How long will it take?" Colby asks, but no one answers him.

"Yes, sir, Mr. I., I'm ready to take you there *anytime*," the captain says in what Colby thinks is a caricature of darky talk. He even hunches himself a little further towards the ground. Then he suddenly rushes the rowboat into the wa-ter; it is done so quickly Colby suspects he and I. have been on many previous expeditions. There is no talk of time, there is no talk of money. The caked and blackened rowboat, full of holes (Colby fears) bobs against the cobbles as the old man wades out and tinkers with the outboard motor. A minute later, he steadies the boat and urges the two men to climb in.

I. leaps delicately from dry land and lands in the boat without wetting his sneakers. Colby, in his hiking boots, blunders into the water and arrives onboard soaked to the knees.

"Good Christ," he mutters.

"Sit down, you're rocking the boat," I. orders. "Now take off those clodhoppers and empty the water out and wring the bottoms of your jeans."

"I'll just leave them on, they'll dry soon enough," Colby says, aggrieved.

But I. is leaning forward to unlace the boots, so Colby is forced to take action.

Meanwhile the captain has satisfied himself that the motor will make one last trip; he hops into the boat and begins to pull violently on the cord. The motor struggles, coughing and balking, finally catches with a sinister low hum as though the cord has pierced a vital organ; throbbing and bubbling, the rowboat plunges sideways into the hurrying river.

"Good Christ," Colby whispers again as an enormous mass of driftwood, the size of the boat, neatly sideswipes them, then hurries on. The captain seems unconcerned; one hand on the tiller, he is looking across at the Indiana shore, where the second largest clock in the world raises its white face, a manmade moon.

"Where are we going?" Colby asks I. in an undertone, circumspect as though they are being hijacked.

"Fountain Ferry," I. says.

"I thought it was closed up, gone."

"Closed up for years now but not gone. They're getting ready to restore it. Going to make a kind of amusement park Williamsburg out of it. Before that happens, you should have a look."

Colby is facing out into the rank river wind. He smells catfish and low-water mud. The captain, behind him, hunches over the motor and fixes his eyes on a tow which is passing uncomfortably close, easing its way down the channel. Colby sees the sinister low wash in front of the barge and thinks of Huck and Jim diving under the paddle wheel.

It turns out the captain has timed it perfectly; the tow passes, its wash just touching and moving the rowboat along.

The island, belted with walnuts and twig-fingered beeches, comes up in front of them suddenly. It is less than a mile long and only a few hundred feet wide; once there was a cornfield in the center and, even earlier, the stockade from which the city sprung.

The captain drives the rowboat into a slot in a black wooden dock, split and heaved by winter ice; there is just enough solid planking left to provide I. and Colby with a footing to get to shore. The captain is tying up the rowboat, promising to wait until they are ready to go back. Colby, for the last time, thinks of saying he doesn't want to stay too long but is shamed out of it by the angle of I.'s rush to the shore.

They step off the dock and find themselves at the start of a thin path through tall grass. Others have been here, boys —

Colby imagines — come off of boats in the summer. The grass is as high as his shoulders, bleached dry and beginning to topple; it will be sickled by the first hard frost. Over the grass, Colby sees a clump of walnuts which must mark the center of the island.

Then Colby sees two tall white posts, decorated with festoons and cupids and garlands. The paint is faded to a tender pink. Gold glints here and there on the garlands. Above the posts, a plank shaped like a flowing banner reads, in pale pink icing script, FOUNTAIN FERRY PARK.

"Was there ever a ferry?" he asks, dazed.

"Yes, it used to bring people from the foot of Fourth Street, on Saturdays and Sundays."

There is a new chain-link gate between the posts, but clever hands have taken the gate from its supports and Colby and I. are able to squeeze through.

They come out on a broad avenue. Even in dereliction it has style. They start towards a far-off edifice which, Colby realizes, is a roller coaster gone down at one end. The high white arches remind him of viaducts he has seen in photographs of Italy.

I. and Colby walk towards this wonder. On either side of the broad avenue, the shaky frame structures of the old amusement park gape in disarray; long narrow buildings that housed the games of chance, their signs hanging down over windows or doors, restaurants and, in the center of the left-hand row, the open sandy space that was used for a beer garden. Colby stops here.

"I remember asking my father where they got the white sand. I never saw white sand before. The river sand is brown."

The white sand, sprouting weeds but shining, reminds Colby of the actual taste of that day, the feverish stomachache excitement — a trip to the city with his father. They were up before light, drinking the cold coffee his mother had left for them, too impatient even to heat it up; dressing side by side in the kitchen in order not to disturb her, washing in cold water from a bucket on the back porch. Colby does not remember ever seeing his father shave or brush his teeth and recalls only once seeing him stripped naked, bathing in a tin tub in front of the fire — "Get out of here before I skin you" — but Colby had already seen enough, for his father is a big man, long-legged and long-armed, with a spider's small body slung between those limbs; he has a small head, too, when his shaggy hair is plastered down with water — five limbs and an ancillary trunk and head: he is here, on the island.

"We sat over there and my father had a beer," he tells I. "It was the only time I ever saw him drink. After that he ordered some potato salad for me. That was something I was used to at home, but this had mustard on it, it burned my mouth, choked me, and he laughed when he saw me forcing it down. I never dared to leave any food on my plate."

I. asks, "Did he take you on any of those rides?"

"Are you kidding? They cost money. He told me we didn't come here to waste money. I don't know what we came for. He was staring around over the one beer, he had a gleam in his eye. I think he'd heard something, at home, about this place, about it being loose, and that excited him. You know he drove me so hard — he was a miner, those years, before he got into the law and took the other side — and the only claim he had on happiness came from those times when, as he called it, he was 'a little wild.'"

"I thought he didn't drink," I. says.

"Well, he didn't. At least I never saw him drink much. 'A little wild' was those times he beat up on my mother."

I. is hurrying ahead. "I want to show you the roller coaster."

"Did I tell you he worked in a mine? The seam so low he used to bump his back on the ceiling? He couldn't wear a shirt, it was too hot, and after a while, he got what he called buttons down the back — a scab on each vertebra."

I. says, "I thought he was a lawyer."

"He was, later, he saved enough and went to Lexington to college — that's where he met my mother — and later on to law school."

"Well," I. says, hurrying ahead, not listening.

As they come nearer to the tumbled white arches, Colby says, under his breath, "He did give me money for that, the roller coaster, and I was scared to ride it; I knew I had to, though, and they put me in the front car. I didn't have sense enough to move further back. Look at that ramp!" he cries, for it is still standing — the long chute which started the train of cars hurtling on its way. "I remember coming down that ramp, my hair blown out straight behind me, my ears pasted to the sides of my head. I was holding on to that front bar — the saliva whipped out of my mouth — knowing I was going to vomit, trying to hold it back, and then the shame, the relief of letting go, vomiting all over my knees, hearing somebody behind me curse. After I got off, I went down to the river and washed it off my pants, but then I had to take my pants off and hang them on a branch to dry. It took some time. When I finally got back to my father, he was furious."

I. says, "Let's climb up in it, it's safe, I've done it before."

"He was back in the beer garden then, but he hadn't been there when I left," Colby says, following I. up the rickety wooden steps. He stops on the platform at the top and looks down the long curve. It does not seem so high now. "When he gave me the money for this ride — it was a nickel, I believe — we were outside a place with red curtains and pictures painted on big pieces of canvas — blond-headed women with big eyes, their eyes took up most of their faces. Well, when I came back in my dried pants he was in the beer garden again. 'Where have you been?' et cetera. No more to say." He watches I., inching out along the track. "What the hell?" he asks, after a time.

I. is halfway down the chute, clinging to the sides with both hands, inching his feet along. "I just want to get to that first platform." He speaks in a conversational tone which nevertheless carries. Colby watches, fascinated, not really afraid for I., who clearly knows what he is doing; he feels each spot with the tip of his sneaker before he places his weight on it. So he inches along. On the first platform where, Colby remembers, the cars paused for a sickening moment before plunging down, I. hallos up, makes victory signs and then drops down a ladder to the ground.

Colby turns around and starts back down the steps. He is feeling cool; the slight breeze has dried his shirt on his back, and he realizes that, while he was talking, he began to sweat.

"I seem to be cut off from my body," he says to I. at the

bottom, and I. laughs, his pale face tiger-striped from the shadows cast by the roller-coaster tracks. "Even when I come —"

"Let's not talk about that. Let's not and say we did," I. says, then starts off in another direction, leaning forward, thrusting his way. Colby, a little cowed, follows him.

"You been here often?" Colby asks.

"Often."

"Who'd you take with you?"

"Nobody."

Colby is reassured.

Now I. is cutting through the long grass, making his own path, winnowing ahead of himself with his arms. Colby, coming behind him, crackles the grass stems under his boots. The sky overhead has darkened and, in the bluish light, I.'s back looks as thin as a blade.

Suddenly they come out on an edge of sand, the river in front of them.

I. hunkers down. Colby sits beside him and I. begins a long account of his boyhood on a Wisconsin farm, his father reading the *National Geographic* after dinner, the three brothers battling in the shadows of the barn; Colby has heard it before, it is one of I.'s songs, and he does not really listen. Everything is told, he believes, in the way I. can squat with both heels on the ground.

The dark river is rushing past. On the far side, the city raises its three skyscrapers like the fingers of a hand; the old waterfront wharfs and warehouses blink broken windows. The bridge with its heavy traffic to Indiana passes almost over their heads. The hum of the traffic is surly, low.

"Hot," I. says, "for this time of year," and he begins to un-button his denim work shirt. He is down to his white cotton drawers before Colby can begin to be surprised. Then these are off, and he stands up and goes to the thick-looking brown water and walks in up to his knees.

"The current, and it's not clean," Colby says, then calls, "Have you had your typhoid injection lately?"

"I'm not planning to drink it," I. says, over his shoulder.

Colby stands up and takes off his clothes, folding each garment into a neat packet and laying it on the brown sand. Then he walks down to the water and tests it with his right foot. It is warm, tepid almost, sluggish here just out of the whirl of the current. He sees tan particles floating, suspended six inches down. Hesitating, he studies I. from behind, notes that his back is a rack of bones. Then I. begins to skip, slowly, in the water, lifting one foot at a time and clapping his hands; he is a tall bird worshiping the sun, here, under the bridge, besieged by the roar of trucks on the expressway bound for the Midwest.

Colby stares at him. He tries lifting one foot, then the other, to catch I.'s beat, and the older man, hearing the tentative splash, looks back over his shoulder and smiles encourage-ment — a little manic, Colby thinks in a last attempt at ob-jectivity, and then he is prancing in the water too. Maybe this is what I missed all along. Nakedness, warm water, dancing. It seems crazed. He cannot rid himself entirely of his self-consciousness, of his awareness of the trucks passing high overhead. Still he keeps pace with I. for a while. Finally I. stops, turns back to the shore, gets out, stretches himself in the warm sun on the sand.

"Come on, dry off," I. says. "We might as well enjoy the sun while we can. Next month, it'll be cold. I've lost my wife, you've lost your girl. We might as well enjoy the sun."

"How did you know?"

"Your hangdog face."

Colby sits down on the damp sand and looks across at the fallen old city and the new buildings towering above it.

I. begins to sing.

"Oh, it's seven years going and seven coming back,
Hi diddlety day
She called for the 'bacco she left in the crack,
Sing hi de diddledum day."

Colby does not wait for encouragement. He takes up the song.

"The women they are so much better than men,
Hi diddlety day
When they go to hell they get sent back again,
Sing hi diddlety day."

Then they are quiet for a while. Finally I. declares it is time to go back and stands up, suddenly businesslike, and dresses himself. Colby dresses, too. They make their way back along the edge of the water to the boat, where the old captain is sitting. He is looking in the other direction, towards the amusement park, and when I. puts his hand on his shoulder, he starts, opens his mouth to laugh at his own surprise and reveals that he has no teeth.

They clamber into the boat.

"How's your wife?" I. calls as the old man wrenches at the motor.

He does not answer until he has it going, and then his

voice cuts through the sound. "Stubborn as hell! I told her the last time, Old woman, you got more sense than that. No heat and I told her, winter coming, you won't make it this time. Wouldn't let me near her, wouldn't even let me in the house, I had to talk to her through the screen door. Wouldn't take no money, nothing."

"I didn't know she'd left you," I. said.

"Long time ago. Long time ago." He chants it like the first lines in a song.

I. does not say anything, and Colby thinks he could at least offer his sympathy.

"I told her what'd happen," the captain says. "Thirty-five years married and then this."

"What?" Colby asks, filling a gap.

They are in the middle of the river; the captain maneuvers around a tree trunk which is coming downstream fast. It has a sinister projecting limb, like a shark's fin; Colby sees the trunk slide by, a few inches down.

"Burnt up," the old man says.

"What?" I. shouts. "What'd you say?"

"Those gas heaters — you know, they sell them at Sears, Roebuck — she got one so she could get through the cold weather, afraid the county'd take her if she didn't have no heat. Some rule like that. She had this big dog, Wilson, she called him, got him to keep her company — ugly and wild, wouldn't let anybody in the house. He knocked it over, I guess."

Colby and I. are both staring at the old man. He is looking ahead, aiming for the dock on the Kentucky shore.

"What?" I. asks again.

"Burnt up," he says. "County come to tell me. Not even enough left to bury."

"Burned up?" Colby asks.

"That heater lit a old piece of rug she had. Flames just went on from there up the wall. The dog got out, went howling around. Middle of the night, nobody to notice. . . . She was under the house, under the floor of the house. Crawled there, I guess, trying to get away from the fire."

"In this town," I. says, "they have nine country clubs, counting the Jewish, they have sixteen marinas, they have a men's club downtown and a women's club at Crescent Hill, the fanciest graveyard in the state, ten health clubs with pools, saunas, exercise devices, six authorized Cadillac deal-erships —"

"The county would have took her. Too damned stubborn. Always was," the captain adds pridefully. "Had a baby once, my son, only one, wouldn't go to the hospital for it, had her old aunt come and catch it — stubborn, stubborn as the devil, paid for it in the end." He crawls to the prow, catches the pier, loops a bit of rope around an upright. "So, gentle-mans . . ."

Colby is feeling in his jean pocket for money.

"He won't take it," I. says, stepping out.

Colby feels that he must give him something because he, Colby, has listened to this story unaffected except by anger at the old man for speaking so calmly, for not allowing the tragedy to be a tragedy, and so must offer him a handful of crushed bills. The captain at first appears not to notice, he busies himself with the rope, retying the knot, then says brusquely to Colby when he keeps on offering, "Take that stuff, white boy. I don't hire this boat to nobody."

Colby goes after I., climbs into the old Pontiac, locks the door, folds his arms. I. glances at him. "Captain tells a different story every time I go over. One time he said it was his daughter burnt up, a whore, served her right, that kind of thing. Another time he told me he never married, never had a child. You can't believe him," I. says forcefully. "You let him upset you, you'll let everybody in the world upset you. Bad for you, when you're trying to deal with that girl. You need all the confidence you can salvage."

"Then why'd you make that speech about country clubs?"

"Because we're responsible for these things, whether they happened or not. They could! The unequal society! You've been so bound up in your own pain — I don't blame you, you have to deal with that, finally — you don't have eyes to see what's going on. There's poverty here, Col, there's people starving, a few blocks from the university. The captain's had a pretty good life, owns his boat, fishes. . . . He knows the way it happens, though, the way it always has, always will, the county trying to take care of people don't want to be taken care of, trying to put them in homes (the irony!) when they just want a chance to live decent, make it on their own."

"What about G.E.? The cigarette place? The distillery?"

"They hire them, they hire them." But then he starts again. "It's hopeless here, Col, it's the old — when they die off, well, maybe then, all right. The busing is getting them an education, you're right, nothing to get so excited about — but have you seen the West End?"

"I haven't seen anything, looks like," Colby admits dismally.

"Don't take it to heart, just take a drive down there someday when you don't have anything better to do, after your girlfriend's gone —"

"Gone!"

"Well, Col, she'll be moving on. You know that. Her life's in the theater."

They were driving under the giant legs of the interstate.

"We haven't even talked about her yet," Colby says.

"Now listen, she told us at breakfast she'd be going on down the river as soon as the play closes."

"All right," Colby says. "All right. Just don't rub it in. The unequal society," he rages. "The unequal part is that some have the gall and others don't."

"You're right, she has it," I. says. After a while, he asks Colby, "You want to marry her?"

"God, no. What kind of a wife —"

"Not the cooking kind. So you're not serious."

"Serious! Never so serious —"

"There's only one serious," I. says. "Either you want to take her for good, or you don't."

"Cut and dried. I don't have that option, anyway."

"Don't weasel out. Your wife was a wife, right, not much of a person, maybe, maybe kind of mean, even, but she knew her place, her role, as they say, she knew she had to please you to earn her keep. I mean you had a contract."

Colby is storming. "That's about all we had! Not even written."

"Well, I know that, but written or not, you had it and you counted on it. That's why I say you're not serious now. Look, you want me to pity you a little, isn't that right, Col, in love at your time of life, in your position, but you're not serious, Col, you're not serious, and you want me and Martha —"

"Goddamn it all to hell," Colby shouts, stomping the car floor, "you have an answer for everything! I've only known her four days!"

"All right," I. says mildly and stops for a light. A pickup of country people is watching them from the other lane. "All right, don't excite yourself. In another day, maybe you'll know." He is about to make one final point, looks at Colby's face and desists. "You want the theater?"

"I'll walk from here," Colby says; his throat scorches with rage. He is afraid he will break down completely, throw a tantrum, if he doesn't escape from the car. "Good-bye," he says, getting out, slamming the door, rushing across the street in front of the pickup of country people, who stare at him as though this is just what they've been told to expect in Louisville.

He looks back to see I. staring, too, his face pale, disturbed.

Colby grinds his fists into his eyes.

Serious . . .

"You like my money," his wife said one night when he screwed her in a way she didn't approve. Usually she initiated intimate contact, designed the position, got it over with neatly; that one night, he flipped her on her stomach and screwed her hard from behind because he didn't want to see her face. "You like my money," she said when finally she was free to turn over. "Isn't that so, Colby?"

Of course he liked her money. Of course! What else did she offer?

Still he slapped her twice, across one cheek and then across the other, knocking her head from side to side on her thin neck: his father throwing his mother against the wall —

it was all coming back, or going to, it was just a question of time. . . . Let me love somebody, if it's a dog or a cat, let me love something I don't want enough to harm . . .

Now hating I. for daring to tell him the truth.

He stumbles past the topless shoeshine show — twenty giant screens, adult entertainment, you must be eighteen to enter, give a gift certificate to a loved one; the windows are covered with drawn organdy curtains as though to conceal the bedrooms of virgins. Further up the street, a low motel promises closed-circuit TV in every room. He sees the back of the Ten-Cent and hurries.

He rams his hands against the push bar on the door and feels it resist. He pushes again as in a fairy tale with the might of ten, even kicks the door with his boot. Well. Nobody home. He checks his watch, turns to compare its out-of-meaning time (two forty-five, what is two forty-five?) with the hands on the daisy clock. The daisy has all her petals open and he sees with surprise that her time agrees with the time on his watch.

Now he realizes that this is real time and that he must find a pay telephone and call to ask I. to cover for his three o'clock class. He shuffles into the booth on the corner, dials and leaves unambiguous word with the English Department secretary: YOU WILL BE SAVING MY LIFE. He can hear the anxious squeak in the woman's voice — this is unheard of, unheard of, she would say if she was higher up on the totem pole — and slams the telephone onto its hook. For once to risk all. He laughs.

Going back to check the Ten-Cent once more, he sees a sign taped to the window. "Rehearsal at Christ Church, 2nd

and Liberty. BE ON TIME PLEASE." He rearranges his expectations, remembering the big Episcopalian mother lode,
its Gothic tower one of the landmarks of the city.

He must hoof it to Liberty unless by some miracle the city
bus happens to pass; he has never had the patience to figure
out its schedule and is resigned to shank's mare when he
hears the bus wheezing behind him. It opens its door in a
mildly predatory way. He leaps in.

Two black women riding to late jobs in the suburbs (no
kids at home) stare at him from a front seat on the bus.
Working along the rows towards them, Colby realizes from
their expressions that he is looking wild. He always sits by
black people, on principle — one of his tiny ways of balanc-
ing his lack of conviction. He sits down on the seat in front
of the pair of women and begins to listen to their conversation.

They do not trouble to lower their voices, and he wonders
after a while if they are troubling to change even one word.
They are droning on and on about female problems, and
now that he is in the way of recollecting, the dim sound of
their voices revives a memory of his mother, strapped inside
a blue blanket, an edge pulled up over her head like a hood,
carried down the path from the house to the handsome
white-and-silver ambulance. She had some kind of bleeding,
not visible on the surface of her skin. No one wanted to discuss it, and Colby had sense enough not to pry.

He jumps off the bus at the corner of Second and Liberty
without having entirely forgiven the women for introducing
that memory; what is it about time and carelessness which
allows memories to reappear like dinosaur bones disgorged

at the base of a fleeing avalanche? His have been buried that long, and he sees little point in dredging them up. After all, she is dead. His mother is dead. There is no way to right that wrong.

Will he ever be able to forgive his father? He does not want to have to face that as an isolated question. When he sees his father's face, feels his father's long wedge of a hand on his shoulder, he will decide through a combination of fear and inertia, decide, probably, to forgive him because that requires no feat, no physical effort, no imagination.

He hurries up the broad shallow steps, then pauses to raise his head and look at the crisp facade of the old church, its round stained-glass window dark behind a mesh of protective wire. Pushing open the door, he smells floor polish and ammonia and sees a light burning, dimly, at the far end of the chancel. It is the hot red eye over the altar. He remembers his mother's hand closing on his shoulder — "Shush! Shush!" — when she took him once secretly to the big church in Lexington. As a girl, she sang in the choir there. They stopped inside the doors — Colby knowing they didn't belong — and he saw the red light and felt his mother's grip. That was where God lived, the God who punished everyone he saw. His mother told him this God has eyes in the back of his head, and Colby, the secret petty thief, secret small liar, secret part-time masturbator, drew from that warning a picture of a bald-headed man with an extra set of glaring eyes in the ridges on the back of his skull. Later, when his mother tried to teach him about the Trinity, Colby was confused because four eyes could not be equitably shared among three. So he grew up in the rank fringes of religion, reluctantly overhearing and unwillingly remembering his mother's whispered instructions.

"Turn the other cheek," she advised him once when he complained of trouble in school, but he knew that only meant bruises evenly distributed — saw that proved on his mother's face.

He thought of that, years later, watching peaceful demonstrators in Chicago being kicked and beaten, knowing there is nothing so tempting as a passive victim. It almost goes against nature, he thinks, to resist that kind of opportunity.

Now he walks unwillingly towards the red light at the end of the chancel, remembering his mother's theories about the state of grace: surely he is not in it now, he has been bustled and elbowed out of it by his appetites. After a while, it dawns on him that he is in the wrong place.

Of course they are not rehearsing in the church itself. There must be a parish house with a basement, an auditorium.

He fishes around through two sets of back stairs and several cream-colored passageways, all smelling of floor wax, with a mysterious green stripe leading along the walls. Finally he hears voices and descends another flight of stairs into the pitch dark. He feels his way towards a door, opens it and pitches into brilliant light.

"Who have we here?"

He blinks around and sees he is on a stage. Several strangers stand in position around him; they break and come towards him warily. "Who have we here?" the dry voice repeats from the darkness in front.

"Colby," Ann Lee says, close to him, and he feels her hand on his arm, guiding him out and down.

"What in the name are you doing here?" she asks when she has him down the steps and sitting in the front row. "Never mind — don't tell me now," she says, and skips back up onto the stage.

"Good morning, Mr. Winn," the dry voice says, and Colby turns to extend his hand into the dark. It is taken and lightly squeezed. Collecting himself, he realizes that it is Grant Tom behind him in the dark and wonders if the man will ever learn to resent him.

"Begin again from 'All I want is a decent life,'" the director says.

Colby hears Ann Lee's clear, almost colorless voice, pure, tranquil, unaccented, not even underlined: "All I want is a decent life."

He blinks up at the stage. She is standing there in her usual clothes, her fringed blue jeans and sagging white sweater, and yet her voice has great authority and the way she is resting her hand on the back of a folding chair as though doing it a favor reminds Colby of one of his mother's compliments: "One of nature's gentlemen." It seems that she has not learned any of this but rather that she has slipped in front of him into another form of herself.

The man who is facing her begins to speak, and Colby burns his eyes to take him in because he is facing Ann Lee and speaking to her and standing maybe two feet away.

"I want to help you. You never have spent the night alone," the man says, reaching out and touching Ann Lee's bare arm.

"I'll learn."

"I want to stay with you till you get yourself back on your feet."

Ann Lee says, "I don't need you," and she reaches up as though to unbutton a jacket. She flings it off, and Colby starts up out of his seat. He has never seen her use a gesture of such carefree intimacy. Everything is told by that gesture. Her eyes are on this man.

"Move just a touch towards him when you say that, Annie," the director instructs. "Remember you are saying one thing and meaning another."

Ann Lee with a thrust of her foot closes up the space that divides her from the stranger.

Colby turns to question the darkness. "Does she really need to . . . ?"

There is a terrible resounding silence. Colby is aware of having, finally, transgressed; he is in no-man's-land now, about to be expelled. He pulls his neck in, hunches his shoulders, slides down into his seat. Nothing is said. Nothing happens.

He begins to study Ann Lee at her angle above him — her ankle, her knee, her arms hanging down her sides — to analyze the intensity of her reaction to this man, this stranger, to master through analysis the pain.

Another man speaks, and then two women, but what they say is without importance. Then Ann Lee begins again: "I'm not going to . . ." There follows a brief exchange and then a hurt flare of rage and she walks a little apart. Colby sighs. All he asks is that she should be surrounded by a little space.

His respite is brief. The director speaks again, methodically creaks in his chair, and Ann Lee moves to within touching distance of the stranger.

Then, like a midnight terror, it passes: lights go on, the director and other people in the audience who have been hidden by the darkness emerge, and Colby, looking around, meets their smiles. He stands up. Apparently he is becoming a fixture. The director tells the people on the stage to take a ten-minute break and then stares at Colby, tapping a pencil in his palm. Colby ducks his head. Nearby the playwright is rapidly scribbling in a yellow pad; she looks up inquiringly but then goes on with her work, and Colby, watching her, is frightened.

Grant Tom leans over the seats between them and asks, "Care for a cigarette?"

"I don't smoke."

But he follows Grant Tom outside.

Grant Tom fishes in his pocket for cigarettes, comes up with a crumpled pack, extracts one and lights it with the last flare of a disposable lighter, which he flings in a frog-shaped litter can. Colby says meekly, "I never was sure what those were for." Grant Tom does not reply; he seems beyond charming. He stands looking down the street and dragging on his cigarette.

"You like to see her onstage?" he asks finally.

"No," Colby says.

"Why do you come, then?"

"Because otherwise I wouldn't see her all day."

Grant Tom nods. "You're hooked, huh?"

Colby sighs.

"All right, you're hooked — you want to be near her. I know this girl, she was down here last spring for six weeks — she didn't tell you that? She did LuAnn in the trilogy for me, I'm surprised you didn't see her. A good actress. One of the best. A real pro, in spite of the way she comes on like a child. Listen to me for your own good. She's a gypsy."

"I know that."

"I should throw you out of rehearsal for talking."

"I know that, too."

"You in pain?"

Colby shrugs, looks at the ground, too close to tears to speak.

"I wish you smoked," the director says.

"Gave that up long time ago. My dad smokes," Colby manages to croak.

The director claps him on the shoulder. "I don't know what to do with you. I'd throw you out if I had any sense. How can it help to see her this way?"

"It doesn't," Colby says, "but I have to."

"I was hooked once in my life, and if it has happened to you, you can see the marks of the beast on somebody else. It was the woman I married, and she led me a dance, screwed around with every lead in every show I ever had anything to do with. I used to spend rehearsals watching to see how she was going to get it started. An actress, gifted, too. She lives abroad now, I haven't seen her in six years. What about a beer? No, we don't have time for that, I told them ten minutes. Maybe a drink, later on? We can go to the Dutch place across the street, it's not too bad."

Colby wants to nurse his wound and knows that shame and pride will keep him from displaying it at the Dutch place; what could be more ridiculous than a raw wound of jealousy in the red plush twilight of that martini palace?

"I've got to get out to the university," he says.

"Let me advise you — avoid the last act. You won't like what you see."

"I came to see."

"Then remember, will you? It's just theater."

"I haven't been able to remember that since the horror movies. My father used to take me. Big blobs of plastic blooming into human babies: 'It's just a movie, it's just a movie,' I used to say to myself, with my hands over my ears and my eyes wide open. Couldn't bear to miss a thing."

The director laughs, holds the door open for him.

In the auditorium, the cast is standing around on the stage. Now that the lights are up, Colby sees that the floor of the stage is marked with white lines; he understands that they represent doors, windows — the set which will be constructed next week. He notices, too, the shabby squat armchairs and the weak-kneed tables; everything is there to represent something else. He thinks, to distract himself, that Ann Lee, too, is there to represent something else: the woman just out of prison. It is only her flesh and bones he is seeing on the stage. This childlike explanation gives him a childlike satisfaction.

"All right," Grant Tom says, "let's go," and he sits down beside Colby in the third row.

The large black-bearded man with whom Ann Lee has been talking steps off a bit, glances at Grant Tom and then at the script in his hand.

"Get those lines down tonight, Marston," the director says.

"I've had the flu. . . . All right." Suddenly the quivering insect voice delves deep into the actor's chest and comes up transformed. He looks at Ann Lee. "I'm going to stay here with you till you get yourself settled. Ain't a thing you can do about it." Into his black beard, he laughs a small laugh.

"Cut the laugh," the director says. "You're meant to be a threat."

"OK," Marston says, scowling.

"Go on."

"I'm going to lay down here right beside you on the bed and make sure nothing happens to you I don't want to happen . . ."

As he speaks the lines, the big man advances towards Ann Lee, who leans back weakly as though to find support in the air. Her long hands are working in front of her ineffectually.

"Please leave me alone . . ." Her voice is ghostly, wan.

Marston puts two heavy hands on her shoulders, and she seems to cave in under the weight. Then he puts his arms around her so swiftly that Colby's peep of outrage is drowned in the rush of the motion. Colby is beating his palms on the back of the seat in front of him, and Marston is kissing Ann Lee's mouth as though he will eat it.

Grant Tom grabs Colby's arms, forces him back down in his seat. "I told you," he hisses.

When the kiss finally ends, Ann Lee comes to the footlights. Her face is calm and white. She peers out into the darkness. "You'll have to make Colby leave," she announces.

Grant Tom says, "I'm keeping him quiet, now. Have a heart."

"Make him leave."

"He's going to behave — aren't you, Colby?"

Colby cannot reply.

"No, no!" Ann Lee shouts. "He's not going to behave. He's a fool. He makes me ashamed!"

Colby stands up. "This is the theater, I know," he says woodenly. "I just want to say, it's so cheap, so terribly cheap. People have to work to make things happen. Don't tell me it's not kissing, it is kissing, and it's for free, and people have to work for that, they have to give up their lives and souls for that, or live in loneliness. Why should it happen on the stage, for free?" Then he turns aside in shame at his own naïveté — from what pocket of his past has that bruised cry risen? — and stares at Grant Tom, hoping to be saved.

Grant Tom sighs. "I'm sorry, Col, you're upsetting her, we have to get through the rest of this scene."

Colby drops into his seat. "I'm not leaving. You'll have to pry me out of here by force."

Ann Lee, on the stage, is shaking her head and swearing.

Grant Tom says, "Just leave for half an hour, let us get to the end of this scene. You're wearing out my patience, Col. . . . Leave!"

At the crack of authority in the director's voice Colby stands up, but as he slides out of the row he sees or thinks he sees a snigger cross the big actor's face. He is on the stage in an instant, his body straining with the sudden effort like a tree in a high wind; he is already panting with exertion when he seizes the big soft man around the middle and begins to haul him to the edge of the stage. The big soft body offers little resistance although the actor's mosquito voice is railing over his head and other people are moving towards them. Colby dumps the actor over the edge of the stage.

"Leave before I call the police!" Grant Tom shouts.

Marston is looking up from the floor where he is sprawled. He looks as if he will cry.

Ann Lee, somewhere, is laughing.

Colby turns to face her defiantly. "So I bother you, I'm a fool, I won't let you get on with your rehearsal."

Below him, the playwright and a young man are helping

the big actor to his feet, brushing him off and soothing him with tremulous cooing noises.

"I bother you because I care about you, I can't stand to see the whole of your life acted out there on the stage, it's so cheap, so trivial, so demoralizing . . ."

"Colby, you're a child," she says.

"You won't go to bed with me," he whispers, "you won't be lovers, and then I have to come here and see it all happening for free on the stage."

She wipes the corners of her eyes. "I told you why."

"It's a game you play like all your other games."

"No. I told you, it's serious."

The other people on the stage hear the change in their voices and shrink away.

Colby does not care about their embarrassment. He wants them to hear. He turns to address them and the large empty house, which he cannot see in the darkness. "I'm in love with you, I love you, I want you, you're not going to be able to get away from me like this — serious, not serious, too serious, it's all shit. Gypsy, gypsy," he says, "you're not going to be gypsying anymore."

She laughs, a high bark, throwing her head back, putting her hands on her hips. "I warned you. I warned you! My father lured my mother out of a swamp with a peppermint stick! It won't happen to me."

Below them Grant Tom says, "Get out of here, Colby. If you know what's good for you, get out and stay out. I think he's sprained his wrist."

Colby notices Marston delicately folding and unfolding his hand.

"Sprained his wrist, that old bluff —" But he begins to scoot towards the door.

It is not a dignified retreat, and yet it is the retreat of a warrior.

Ann Lee leans out from the stage, watching him go — some sort of princess leaning out from her tower. The house-lights flash on to illuminate Colby's departure, and he turns at the door to give her a last forbidding stare.

"I'm coming to get you at six o'clock!"

"No."

"Six o'clock!"

He bangs out the door.

13

LATER, in the Weeklys' kitchen, Colby is standing by the stove watching Martha, who is watching Ann Lee sitting with the baby across her lap; the baby has gone to sleep between bouts with the bottle, which Ann Lee insists she must have now and then to begin the process of weaning. Martha has accepted this verdict, Colby thinks, with unusual placidity; Ann Lee explained that the bottle would mean Martha could sleep through the night undisturbed, but this has not happened yet. Ann Lee says that Martha is still up all night long, padding down the hall in her flat pink slippers and mossy-looking flannel robe, as though she is looking for a lost soul.

The baby wakes with a start, and Ann Lee plunges the rubber nipple into her mouth before she can make a sound. "She's not starving to death, I can tell you that," she reminds Martha. "She's already taken more than half the bottle." At that the baby's round heavy head falls back the full length of her stalk neck; she is asleep as suddenly as if she has been poleaxed, and Ann Lee says, "Let her lie here awhile till the milk settles and then you can take her up and put her to bed — no cuddling in your own bed. I know you. You ought to think more about poor I."

"I. is working on a poem," Martha says, "and I only cuddled the baby in bed that once."

"Once is already enough. Where I come from, they roll on them — the mothers, I mean; like a sow on her farrow." Ann Lee examines the baby's face, then darts her up against her shoulder and begins to pat her back firmly. "Looks like a bubble." The sleeping baby's face contorts, her body twists, and a loud burp erupts but does not disturb her sleep.

"Now, then." Ann Lee lays the baby back down on her knees.

Colby says, "I want to ask you, Martha, can you do without this girl here for the weekend? I want to take her out, show her some of the state."

Ann Lee says, "That's the first I've heard of it."

Martha says, a little too quickly, "Why, of course, Colby. Do you want to leave tomorrow?"

"Now wait a minute here," Ann Lee says, sounding uncertain. "I'll have to think about it. You can't just go and make up my mind for me like that."

"I thought you said you wanted to see the mountains."

"Well, one day."

"Tomorrow is going to be the day," Colby says.

"When did you hatch this scheme?" Even as she frowns at him, her lips are twitching.

"When I threw that damn fool off the stage. Have to get you away from that kind of trash, show you some real people."

"It turned out he sprained his wrist."

"Caught his whole considerable weight on it: I thought actors are supposed to know how to fall. Know how to fall or lose weight!"

"He was going to sue this fool," Ann Lee tells Martha. "It took Grant and me the rest of the afternoon to argue him out of it. You've got a friend in Grant," she tells Colby.

Martha exclaims, "My Lord, Colby, you used to be so opposed to physical violence!"

"That guy was taking advantage."

"Just playing his part," Ann Lee says. "I dread to think what Colby would do if he saw what comes next. Abe puts his heart into it."

Martha says, "They won't be inviting you to any more rehearsals."

"That don't matter none," Colby says, imitating. "I did what I had to do. Anyway, I'll have her to myself, Saturday and Sunday."

"That'll mean missing a rehearsal," Ann Lee says. "I'll have to ask."

"Yes, you talk to Grant Tom. You talk to him right now. He lives in the Highlands, doesn't he?" Colby has seized the telephone book.

Martha, under cover of the excitement, slips the baby off Ann Lee's knees.

"Careful, you'll wake her," Ann Lee says even as she shakes her head at Colby and tries to get at the telephone book. "You are not going to disturb Grant Tom this late at night."

"If you leave it till tomorrow, you won't do it." he is leafing through the T's, now and then raising the telephone book over his head to get it out of Ann Lee's reach.

She subsides finally and notices that Martha has gone off with the baby.

"You'll wake her up if you change her now," she shouts after her.

Colby is dialing. The blurred voice on the other end is not familiar, and he asks, crisply, for the director. It turns out that it is Grant Tom, who has answered out of a couple of hours of sleep. "Yes . . . What you want? . . ."

"Ann Lee, for the weekend. Don't say no. It's a bargain. You'll be getting rid of me at the same time."

"My God, Colby Winn, whoever put you on the same side of the earth? . . . Don't you know the kind of trouble you've caused already —" And, fully awake, he is rattling on; Colby holds the receiver away from his ear and winks at Ann Lee. Now and then he puts the receiver back against his ear and says, "Yes?" Once he apologizes. After a while, the director calms down.

"You can't have her," he says, into Colby's silence.

"Well, I'm going to take her anyway. You want to fire her? You'll never find another leading lady in this town. Look at the two sticks you have to put up with for her sisters, you'll have three sticks if you let Ann Lee go — even this hick town won't tolerate that. You'll have that little sweat bee that reviews for the paper down the back of your neck."

There is another diatribe; Colby holds the receiver towards Ann Lee so she can judge the director's falling crescendo. "Pretty good?" he asks.

"Grant Tom, I'm helpless," Ann Lee calls towards the receiver. "I'm in this guy's power!"

Then she snickers, yawns and stretches.

Finally Colby decides to end the game. He says into the receiver, "She'll be there for the morning rehearsal on Monday, and when you decide on the time, please call and leave word at the Weeklys'. You got the number?" And although he knows Grant Tom is not even trying to scrape up a pencil and paper, he tells him the number, twice. There is some further commotion about a costume fitting which Ann Lee will be missing and after dealing with that and hanging up, Colby says, "Why does he hire a star if he doesn't want star behavior? Now you are going to have to control him tomorrow morning when he starts to work on you; you already have your line, just repeat it — you're in my power." Colby puts his hands, lightly, around her throat.

Then he begins to close. He feels, under his thumbs, the knot in her throat and, against his fingers, the cords in the back of her neck. At first he rubs his fingers over those cords and then he clamps down firmly on them. He feels the knot in her throat jump and then she raises her hands and begins to pry at his hands. He tightens his hold slightly. Her neck is so thin. Her fingernails scrape against the backs of his hands and he sees her knees jump and is glad the baby is gone. Softly, he tells her that she must come with him, that he is not going to let her go. Her fingernails scrape lightly, he cannot believe that her strength is so diminished; perhaps she assumes he is just playing a game and he tightens his hold just a little to show her that, in fact, he can do anything with her he wants. Then he lets go.

Ann Lee coughs dryly and jumps up and runs to the sink and splashes water into her mouth with her hand. When she turns to deal with Colby, her face is wet and flushed and her eyes are bright as though with the reflected light of a fire. Reflected light. Reflected glory. Colby can't believe what he has just done. He has never seen his strength transferred like this.

"What's the matter with you? . . . Trying to scare me. Thinking you can scare me like that . . ."

"Weren't you?"

She considers, feeling her throat with her fingers.

"I was just about to be . . ."

"Next time, I'll hold on longer. Or harder."

He is laughing. Ann Lee says, "I'm not scared of you," and she begins to fold a heap of clean diapers. Now and then she reaches up reflectively and touches her throat. "You can't hurt me," she says.

Colby hears that she wants to believe this, that she will continue to test the truth of this statement. He sits down in a chair and watches her. The scene is colored and shadowed in a way he remembers: the glaring light from the overhead bulb, the thicket of shadows cast by the kitchen chairs, raked back from the table at odd angles, the checked dishrag hung over the faucet to dry. This is the kitchen after the day is over. The scene for scenes. He watches Ann Lee's buttocks move inside the sheath of her gray skirt and thinks of pushing her down on a chair but knows she will scream loud enough to bring Martha. He has pushed her as far as he wants to push her, for tonight.

Later, going out to get into his car, having claimed his one kiss and laid his hand for an instant on her waist, he remembers that other kitchen. His mother's kitchen, where the tall blue wooden chairs threw a thicket of spindly shadows against the tarnished white wall. His father bent his mother backwards over the sink and she flipped her hands at him, scuttling her fingers across his checked shirt while he pressed his thumbs against her throat and Colby, in the doorway, watched the erection pushing out the front of his father's pants.

He leans against the car, retching, nothing coming up.

Then he sees the light in I.'s study and knows his friend is there, tapping away at a poem. The poem will never be published, no one will read it except for a handful of friends sitting in front of I.'s scuffed fireplace some evening. When it is Colby's turn to write on Melville, the book will be published by a university press and no one will read it, either. Yet when the wind blows, Martha turns to I. and he holds her in his arms.

When did they part ways? Colby thinks it was at Fountain Ferry when I. peeled off his clothes and cavorted in the sun.

For ten years, I have lived without repeating any of this, Colby thinks, as he unlocks his car and climbs in. He sits for a while with his hands on the steering wheel, watching the light go off in the kitchen — Ann Lee has finished her cup of herb tea — and then the light flicks on in her bedroom, upstairs. For ten years, and I can still go on that way. He remembers the peacefulness of those days, the weekend mornings in bed, masturbating, the visions of violence only the weeds of a rational mind.

In lifelessness, anything is permitted. Even the sudden scorching visions were another manifestation of the way a controlled imagination can burst out. Harmless, literary, like his nicely turned metaphors about the writers he admires, which will never affect anyone and do not even affect their author except with a neat little pang of satisfaction, a tiny cerebral orgasm. *Those who can't, teach. Those who can't teach, write. But he can. He can do. He can do and do.*

14

COLBY TEACHES THE NEXT MORNING in a dream. They are having a false spring: the air is warm, soft, nearly watery as it moves slowly in and out of the open classroom window. Colby is not surprised to see that the redhead at the back of the room has at last seized hold of a blond girl's attention. There is copulation in the air, he thinks as he watches the boy place his paw on the little round knee.

The failing of the night before makes Colby unusually gentle. When the acned boy comes up, after class, to ask a question, Colby smiles at him and nearly offers congratulations. It is a moment of happiness, after all. He hopes the two will have a soda together. Then the weather will change and the blond will notice his pimples. Still, twenty years later when there is a spring day in the fall, the carrottop will think, This is the kind of weather she let me touch her knee.

He goes at lunchtime to pick up Ann Lee at the Ten-Cent. She is waiting outside, a sight he never expected to see. Standing next to the big door, her hands in the pockets of a tan jacket, she is placed as though she expects to wait patiently for a while.

He guides her to his car through a cement jungle built for the children of the city; it says so on a book-shaped plaque. "Only used by dogs or drunks," Colby remarks, wishing he could leap in the air and click his heels together. Instead he asks her soberly about her clothes for the weekend.

"You know I travel light."

"Not even your knapsack, this time?"

"You'll buy me what I need, won't you?"

"I'm not even buying you a toothbrush. I refuse to cross that line."

She takes a toothbrush out of her pocket. It is wrapped in a scrap of tissue, which she refolds carefully, and then stows the bundle away. Something in the looseness of her blue jean pocket makes him think she has lost weight.

"You eating anything at all?" he asks as he holds the car door for her. She climbs in, settles herself, smooths the denim over her knees.

"Not much, lately."

"What's the matter?"

"I guess I'm worried."

"Worried?" he asks gaily, backing the car out of the lot, pressing a dollar into the numbed-looking black hand which is extended to him from the wooden shack; then he backs the car fast into the traffic on Third Street.

"I don't know what's happening to you, Colby," she says.

"You mean last night?"

She is silent. After a while, she says, "I thought at first you might be a nice person."

"I am a nice person till you make me mad," he says, willing her to accept his childishness. "Look at that!" he adds as they flash past a converted pool hall. TOPLESS SHOESHINE GIRLS!" The blacked-out window is decorated with a sketch of a man sitting in a chair with his feet extended towards a naked woman, kneeling, a brush in her hand.

"They think of everything," Ann Lee says.

Colby understands suddenly that he is going to have to explain himself. She has made it clear by her tone that otherwise he will be lumped with the man in the sketch, with the men she imagines inside, swaying and peering at LIVE GIRLS ONSTAGE.

"Look, last night you reminded me —"

"That's no excuse," she interrupts, then adds, "I like you, Colby," and for the first time in their brief acquaintance, she reaches out and touches him with simple affection.

He is shocked. He does not see the connection between whatever it is he has caused her to feel — panic, maybe? — and her endearing action.

Still, her fingers on the back of his hand are warm.

"That feels good," he says as she continues to stroke the back of his hand; but he is angry. He is also getting an erection, and he knows that she sees this and that she is smiling her interior smile.

"I'm going to run off the road," he says. They're waiting for the light at Broadway, and in order to conceal his face, he turns and stares at the hams hanging in COUNTRY FOOD SHOPPE. Next door, an itinerant artist displays his wares in what used to be a chic antiques store, now relocated in the suburbs. The big blurry red and pink nudes of the itinerant sign painter, portrait painter and general handyman of the arts are hung in the windows, flanked by the country hams.

Ann Lee takes her hand away. "It's only affection, Col. I won't go to bed with you, you know. Just want you to know for when we get there."

"Too bad for you, lady. I wasn't counting on it," he says but feels at the same time the terrible drop, the lurch in his stomach which means that at some time in the night, in a dream or a plain piece of sleep, he has begun to count on it. Like for the boy with his hand on the girl's knee, for him it is the weather, only the weather, and the fact that he is in his car, heading out of the city for the weekend; and what has all that got to do with the woman beside him, with the shape of her thighs, with the shape of her expectations? Nothing, nothing. It is the land of dreams.

He drives fast out Broadway, longing to leave the city behind, to peel off the warehouses, the stained political posters: DON'T GRIPE IF YOU DON'T VOTE: can that apply to him? He has not yet changed his registration and doesn't know in all honesty if he will ever bother. He drives through the leaf-strewn Highlands and out along the road past the park, laid out, he tells Ann Lee, by Frederick Law Olmsted. A tornado toppled its highest trees, and now the golf course is as naked as the back of a hand. Two mallards are skimming the surface of the pond which a lone golfer crosses, his pig of a cart hunching across the bridge. "Those forms of life don't intersect," he tells Ann Lee.

"Tell me about your wife," she replies.

Colby takes the chute onto the expressway. "Why do you want to know, all of a sudden?"

"Because I don't understand you."

"I'm not certain I want you to!" But her look cuts across his jocularity; he cannot continue on that note.

"I met her in college," he begins.

"And felt — ?"

"You mean the first time I saw her?"

"Yes."

"She was so thin. So thin and trim. Nearly a boy's body. We were nineteen. No buttocks, almost, although she did have breasts. Have you seen women like that?"

"I'm one, myself."

"No — not fat, you know, but you have something substantial about you . . ."

"Tell me what you felt when you first —"

"She was standing in a room full of people on the second floor — a brick house in Cambridge. The house was for clubs, gatherings, all that kind of thing. This happened to be the time when the literary people gathered. They had a magazine. She was standing under a bulb in the ceiling so the light was flat on her hair. Blond hair, fine, threads really. I thought she stood that way, one hand on her hip, leaning back against a table, like a girl who's grown up with boys. You know what I mean. 'Let them alone, they're just boys.' Tolerance. Latitude. The kind of girl you can put your head down in her lap when you're drunk. I was wrong. Dead wrong. She dressed that way, had that kind of body, but she was an only child, only girl, raised by her father. Her mother died when she was a baby. Raised to be a man's companion — that's different. Besides, her father never drank. He was chairman of the English Department at Harvard, there was even a great-uncle who'd been on the faculty. Distinguished something. I guess it was the distinction. Remember what I came from. I don't want to believe that. . . . Her family had such a hold on the place and I was still getting ribbed be-

cause of my accent — my second winter in Cambridge, and
I still didn't have a topcoat. Not just lack of money. Those
first two winters I went around in a tweed jacket, couldn't or
wouldn't believe in that kind of strong lasting cold."

"You went to bed with her right off?"

"Don't be crazy, that was the fifties, you didn't do things
like that. We saw each other at the literary magazine, she was
writing things, I was 'editing' — taking liberties with other
people's stuff. I was also giving them my poems, which they
wouldn't print."

"I didn't know you wrote poetry."

"I didn't. Don't. Verse. It didn't take much concentration
or spelling or punctuation — that was why I liked it. Do
you know I'm still ashamed of my spelling? We had look-say
early in the mountains, it was supposed to be good for children from bad backgrounds. That means I never will be able
to spell."

"Did they ever print your poems?"

"No, they had better-educated things to do. I mean, mine
were terrible — about fall, spring, love — all that. The truth
was I wanted to forget it — I mean, the flowering Judas, the
mountain laurel — and the quickest way to forget it was to
set it down in those kinds of verses. Clichés kill. Have you
ever noticed how a bad image kills a good image? One bad
apple — that kind of thing. 'Fiction is a barrel,' I ought to
say. Why am I talking on and on like this? Well, anyway, if
you're stuck with the kind of images I was stuck with — my
mother's blue kitchen chairs, for instance — you can get rid
of them by applying some ordinary hackneyed images to
them, kill them off."

"Blue kitchen chairs."

"Everything at home," he says slowly, catching his breath, "happened in the kitchen."

She is silent: a sure instinct not to pry. Colby looks at the vast array of movie houses and department stores they are passing. "The Tombs of the Pharaohs. When they dig up this civilization, they'll find these great shopping centers and think they were temples."

"How soon did you two get married?"

"You must be getting serious about me, asking all these questions," Colby says sarcastically. "It was after graduation, and I hardly touched her all that time. I mean, we had a kind of professional friendship. She took an interest in my awful poems — she never had any kind of taste, except in clothes — and she started to work on them, out of the kindness of her heart, giving my images a little polish. I was grateful for the help because it put the truth, the real look of things, further behind me. Oh I wanted so badly not to remember. Not to feel. The whole point to college was to learn not to feel, and it's true if you get away from sights, sounds, smells, some of the feelings do go, they tend to die down, although there was a cafeteria in Cambridge I never went back to because the spaghetti on the steam table smelled like school. . . ."

"Anyway she finally asked me to marry her."

"She did?"

"You dare to sound surprised. I won't investigate." Again his humor falls into her simple quiet waiting. "She didn't want to live alone, I guess. She certainly didn't want to have to go back to living with her father on Garden Street, where she'd spent her whole life, and he was having a greenhouse built for her, having her study painted robin's egg blue. I knew it would mean a sure place for me, but I said that wasn't what mattered, that I was marrying her in spite of that — the security thing made me mad as hell. But the truth was, of course — you've guessed it — that I didn't think I'd be able to make it up there, alone; I hadn't really found my place there, after four years. I don't mean grades, of course. I could do the work, I was going on to grad school — that wasn't the question. The question was about making it, I mean, becoming one of them instead of an eternal transplant. And I never could have done that on my own. Scholarship boy from Appalachia makes good at Harvard. That was before people got so sentimental about 'the mountains.' I couldn't go far enough, alone. I never would have been given tenure, I would have been stuck at teaching fellow, year after year — the grimy guy in the cafeteria line, old tweed jacket, slight stink of sweat, not quite fitting in, missing it by an inch. She, my wife, used to buy my clothes, a size too big so it would look as though intellectual effort was wearing me down. . . . And her parties, she knew how to do it as though she was just including those men and their wives in our life: come over, just nothing, bring a bottle of wine — but that casual evening would have been planned for days, even the books and magazines on the coffee table would have been through three or four eliminations. Bed doesn't matter much in a situation like that. Too many other things come first. It's a tiresome irrelevancy, like an attack of flu."

"I can't keep up with all that," Ann Lee says.

"Don't keep up, then. Let me talk." He is a horse with the bit in this teeth. "The last straw — by then we'd been married ten years — was when she somehow got pregnant. Neither one of us wanted children. I mean, how could children have made it in that life, that house? There really wasn't an inch of extra room. Besides, I couldn't feel, never have been able to feel what it would have been like . . . I mean, the feeling of one."

Ann Lee says, "What's hard for me is the idea of not having them. That's just an idea. The feel and the smell of them —"

He interrupts, ducking his head to apologize. "I mean, she did get pregnant. Never mind how, she did. She went and had it aborted right away, never told me about it till it was already gone. Too late. Maybe I thought she was lying, sitting there on her couch, her chaise-lounge, filing her nails, telling me the thing was gone. No, she didn't call it the thing. She said, the fetus. Is that closer to human? I don't know. Maybe I didn't want her to have control over her own body, her own fate — that's what women say now — but what I felt then was that she had done it to protect me from one of my few possibilities. You know that kind of fencing in."

"No."

"That was when I told her I was going to leave her, and it was suddenly clear to me that I'd been thinking about it for years; I used to wake up in the middle of the night and wonder what was bothering me; it was that, I was making that speech, planning that getaway. Even when I thought things were all right between us, there was something screaming in my sleep, Not all right, just hell, plain hell — something muscular planning to get out. So the speech came out smooth. She cried and cried and I didn't believe a tear of it — excuse me — but when she made scenes, it was most unconvincing, she was not the sort to puff and snort and that was all she knew how to do to fake feeling — excuse me, that's what it was, I'm being purely objective. The only time she ever moved me, the only time I ever knew for sure she was moved, was when she was standing by the window one Saturday in March and reached out and ran her finger along the venetian blind. Just that."

"Poor woman," Ann Lee says.

"No, she was fine, save your sympathy for me, I can never get enough of it. Then her father tried to lay down the law, called me into his office, spoke to me of my brilliant career — which wasn't turning out to be so brilliant, by the way; I was still stuck with Freshman English — and then hinted to me that if I left his daughter, the doors of the greatest university in this country would be permanently closed to me. So I left. I didn't want to hang around waiting for those doors to close. I mean, he was chairman of the English Department."

They are out in the suburbs now. Colby runs down into silence. The fields along the road are beginning to spread and flatten, the dim sky fades. Far away on the rim of a hill, a tobacco barn shows light through its ribs. They pass a field of black cattle, and then a cornfield laid low by frost. They are out, out and away, and Colby wants to shout at Ann Lee that everything he had been saying is just the past, the dead past, and that they are moving now into a future where there will be a long ribbon of untraveled highways and spreading midwestern fields under a pale sky. They have never found their background before — surely it was not the Ten-Cent, it was not even Timmy's or the Weeklys' house. It is the fields — and he begins again to talk.

"I've always thought if I was going to stay here — and it looks as though I am going to stay here — I'd move out, buy some bottomland by the Kentucky River and set up farming. I know enough from the way I was raised to make a go of it with chickens and hogs, at least."

She says, "I never want to go back up there."

Colby says, "Why not?"

"Oh, Col, it was so poor. You think the mountains are beautiful, but how can you enjoy them when the people are so poor? There's nothing but coal up there, coal and suffering. I don't want to go back into that misery. I was so glad the day my folks decided to move down to Cincinnati, the new road just sort of drew them. I could have kissed every inch of the way. No, I won't go back up there, or even go back to farming somewhere else. I'm a city girl from now on, Col, I know too much about the other way."

"All right, no Kentucky River."

After a minute, she says quietly, "The play opens next Thursday, Col. It'll be on two weeks. Then I'll be going."

He swallows. He has been alertly avoiding calendars. "This is all I ever bargained for," he says, and hates himself for a coward and a liar.

"Now wait a minute." She is looking at him. "This is not going to be as easy as all that!"

"Don't be so sure!" He is furious at her for her condescension and wants to prove that she is nothing to him but the proofs are not available, he is not quick at transferring his feelings and he knows that his scowls are giving her satisfaction.

"I want a Coke," he growls and swerves into a service station.

He has to go to the attendant for change for the machine. Colby looks so sourly at the boy that he retreats into the garage. From inside the doorway, several men watch as Colby slides the quarter into the Coke machine and then begins to wrestle to extract his bottle. The glass door won't open. He pulls at it, the flimsy chrome knob nearly twists off in his hand, but it is locked and his quarter is gone. He jams down the coin return lever, but nothing happens except for a satisfied internal gurgle. Then he pulls back his foot and kicks the machine as hard as he can but it does not flinch, it is impervious.

A large man in jeans and a checked shirt under suspenders leans out of the doorway and asks, "Need help?"

"No!"

At the same time, Ann Lee is passing to the ladies' room. She has to stop in at the station for the key, which she takes away swinging from the ends of her fingers. She is also walking with a certain twitch, and the man in the checkered shirt is staring.

"My, my!"

"Look at that!"

"Who she belong to?" the first man asks with an evil twinkle.

"Go to hell!" Colby shouts.

"Oh, she's yourn? She's riding in your —"

He does not get to the end of the question. Colby in one step has abandoned the Coke machine. Enraged, he reaches out and grabs the suspenders and pulls them, and they are limber, nearly limp; he gathers up the excess in his hands and pulls the man almost nose to nose. The man is taken aback and breathes once, hard, into Colby's face, loses his balance and stumbles against him.

"You don't ask questions!" Colby shouts, astonished by his own strength.

"Hey, what's the matter with you . . ."

Colby lets go of him, and he staggers back, feeling his chest as though something is missing, and then he swings at Colby, his flat hand sliding down through the air. Colby steps aside. The man's hand swings again, falls through the air near Colby's shoulder; they stare at each other. Colby turns and starts back to his car.

Then he remembers that he has failed to get the Coke. He wonders if he will lose face if he goes back to tussle with the machine again. On the other hand, he cannot afford to pretend that he has forgotten his quarter; the suspenders will take that as sure proof that he has lost his nerve. Colby turns around.

The man is still standing a few feet away, humped a little, weaving. "Didn't mean nothing," he says when he catches Colby's eye.

"Go to hell," Colby mutters, starting for the machine. He takes another quarter out of his pocket and slams it into the slot. There is a strange humming sound, as though the machine is considering, and then he hears the tumble of gears. He can feel the hidden catch give as he reaches out and touches the chrome knob. At the same moment, he is struck in the back of the head.

Colby thinks as he goes down that he is prepared for this,

that he will break nothing, spill nothing, just drift off into sleep. He does not fight it, he curls up with his cheek on his hand, he is gone before anyone can come, before Ann Lee can get out of the ladies' room, before the two men in the service station can rush out, before the suspenders can start to explain, a sputter of words, damn fool, pick a fight, see what happens . . .

He is out for the best and shortest moment of his life.

Ann Lee's hands are on his face, he can smell hand lotion and feel the lines and ridges in her fingers. She is smoothing his hair back, feeling all over his face as though she has gone blind. "I can't tell," she mutters.

"I'm all right," Colby croaks, his throat parched, his head aching.

She lifts his head onto something, a mat or a towel which one of the station men has provided; he lets his head hang heavy in her hands, wonders if she guesses at his relief — to lie helplessly curled on his side while she lifts his head onto a towel.

"All right, all right," he croons as she is in the process of straightening out his legs and arms, arranging him for display.

One of the men is explaining something, apologizing. The chief villain has apparently slouched off.

"Never mind," Colby growls through clenched teeth. "Never mind!"

"He's all right," Ann Lee says, sighing.

"Except for my head . . ."

"Well, wallop you pretty hard . . ." They are beginning to see the humor of it; there is a tendency to smirk (he can hear it) now that they know there is nothing seriously wrong.

"You want to try to stand up?" Ann Lee asks.

Before he can decide, she puts her arms around him, heaves until he is sitting up; he wonders why she is willing to touch him in that way, to pull at him with all her strength when she has given up any other kind of touching. "I was a nurse once," she says severely to a man who has dared to advise her not to move him. "Delivered thirteen babies single-handed."

There is a low whistle of approval. These are all family men, they know what it is to be relieved of responsibility.

"All right, now," Ann Lee says. She is all briskness and self-assurance. "You get up and I'll help you to the car. You better let me drive."

"I want my Coke," Colby says. "It's paid for, twice. Get it out of the machine."

He has still not opened his eyes. Someone presses a damp cold bottle into his hand.

"This it?" He has to open his eyes to see. There is a crack of light across his pupils, one terrible dart of pain, and then he is all right except for the ache in the back of his neck. "What'd he do to me?" he asks.

"Swatted you good," one of the men says and, this time, there is cautious laughter.

Ann Lee has passed her arm around his waist. "Lean on me," she orders. Colby leans with all his weight as though to force her down, but she does not even stagger. She takes him with small steps to the car, which is on the edge of the lot, its door open, the motor still running.

She maneuvers him into the passenger seat, checks to see that he has his Coke, then slams the door. She hightails it around to the driver's side. Gets in, then sits bemused. The car is unfamiliar to her, and she shuffles her feet along the floor, feeling for the pedals.

"Why you have to fight . . ."

"I didn't fight."

She starts the car, pulls out onto the highway.

"That all you going to say?" he asks bleakly after a while.

"Yes," she says.

15

A HALF HOUR LATER, they are coming into the foothills, low humps mounting out of the agricultural plain; Colby sees them in the distance with apprehension. It has been twenty-five years since he has been back on this edge of the state. He thinks of his father sitting in his office in Pineville — the only lawyer in town and liking it. At certain times of the year, he hires Miss Mamie Hudson to come and type and answer the telephone — Colby has heard her voice, nasal and refined — and then, when things slacken, the old man lays her off, knowing she will be available the next time he needs her.

"My father's a lawyer, up there in Pineville," he tells Ann Lee, and hears the mountain twist in his voice.

"Let's go see him," she says promptly.

"Come on, now, you don't know what you're saying. This is just plain people, nothing fancy, nothing you'd appreciate."

She glances at him. "I don't know what you're talking about. I'd like to meet your dad."

He slumps down on his spine in the seat. This has been in

his mind since he first suggested the trip; to take her up there and let them stare at each other, see what conclusions they'd draw. (Not that his father would mention them, but Colby thinks he can guess from the way his father sucks his breath in, tips his nostrils, the exact degree of his approval or disapproval.)

"How long has it been since you've seen him?" Ann Lee asks.

"Twenty-five years."

"How come?"

"When I left home, I swore I'd only come back if Mama called me. She did. By then it was too late, she was dying, but I stayed there a week afterwards. He was drunk the whole time, I mean respectable-drunk, going down to his office every day, coming home in the evening, talking about everything under the sun — he wasn't going to have her dying get him down, oh no. The night of the funeral, he brought some girl home, some whore he'd picked up at the café in town, and I got up and went out to my car in my pajamas and drove out of there, shook the dust off my feet. I mean, he is too much," he finishes, trying to lighten the tone. His voice grates.

"We ought to go see him," Ann Lee says, as though it is the simplest thing. "It's not *that* far."

"I'm taking you to Natural Bridge, to the lodge there."

"We could get to Pineville and back to Natural Bridge before night."

He wishes she was not driving. "We could."

"Well?"

He realizes that he will never be able to refuse her.

"I'll have to call the old bastard."

"Why not just drop in?"

"God knows what shape —"

"Why not just drop in?"

"Oh, God," he groans, "I wanted this to be a rest, I wanted this to be a vacation."

She takes a breath. "Vacation from what? Your life's a vacation, Colby."

"Hell!" he says. "Who are you — ?"

"I care about you, Colby."

"Don't give me that kind of care. The only kind of care I want, you can't give."

"I don't call that —"

"Sex! Whatever you call it!" He is shouting. Pain echoes in his head. She continues to drive slowly along, her eyes resting on the horizon over the rim of the steering wheel.

"Listen," she says. "I want you to tell me something. Tell me the truth. When you're pushing me this way, what do you feel?"

"Like murdering you!"

"Is that sex? I'm not talking about love," she adds.

"Whatever it is, it's strong," he says.

"I'm not going to let you get away with that, Col."

"It's strong! What's the matter with that!"

After a while, she asks, "Are we going to Pineville?"

"Yes, we are going to Pineville."

"Isn't this the turn?"

"All right," he says, and feels what he has always dreaded, the great peace and quiet of subjugation, the pleasure of giving up. Why fight? Who is there to fight? A wandering minstrel girl?

They turn off at a junction where machine-made quilts

with peacock designs are strung along a clothesline. "They've been making peacocks since I was little," Colby says. "Somebody came along here a few years back and got the women started making real quilts again, you know, Star of Bethlehem, Marriage Knot — but they send them all to New York, you don't see them at the gas stations."

She says, "I grew up sleeping under a plain old patched quilt my grandmother made out of my mother's baby dresses. Tiny prints, you know, tiny houses and tiny baskets."

They start up their first incline. A truck is laboring ahead of them, shifting gears raspingly. They follow along behind; the road is too narrow to allow for passing.

"How are you getting along with that baby?" Colby asks.

"That baby is fine. I mean, up in the night and all but that doesn't bother me. If mothers would leave babies alone, babies would be fine."

"Well, Martha . . . But I never thought she was the nervous type."

"It's not nerves, it's love," Ann Lee says grimly.
"Maybe it never came out before. I mean, she and I. have a pretty easy life. The worst strain cooking dinner for a visiting poet, would she eat greens. Or maybe a question to do with three months' vacation in the summer when I. is set in his tracks and won't get off them, can't be tempted to the mountains, the sea or a free conference, wants to spend one more hundred-and-ten degree day in that study under the roof, working on one line of a poem, can you say finishing anything?'"

"I thought you liked them."

She steers around a lump of coal the truck in front of

them has spewed out, then says, "Colby, I'm not talking about liking or not liking."

"You sound like you've seen through them, some way."

"I was talking about why this baby is a strain on Martha."

"Well, I haven't seen it. The day she was nursing it in the kitchen —"

"She's fine when she'll let me help. She won't always let me help. You've heard of being jealous."

He watches her press the brake down as the truck in front of them slows to negotiate a right-angle turn. She is wearing her sneakers, and the thin bird bone in her ankle juts over the edge of the shoe.

"I don't know what they're going to do about that baby when I go," she says.

"They'll find somebody else. One of the undergraduates; I mean, there are other people who know about babies."

She smiles. "Yes, but I doubt Martha will let any of them in. She only lets me in because of you. Women will do that. Taking on another women, trusting her on a man's say-so."

"They'll manage," he says.

"Of course they'll manage, but the question is, what will happen to that baby? Martha already has her ready to fuss the minute she sees her. I tell you, a week-old baby can read the expression on its mother's face. She'll stiffen up and start to fuss, right off. Martha'll try to nurse her, think the milk's not what she wants or that there's not enough (one time she wanted to measure it in a measuring cup), then try to get her to watch the mobile — and all that baby is getting all that time, is just the idea that her mother's scared and will do anything to get a little less scared. That's what I call ruining."

Colby says, "I'm jealous. It's childish, but I'm jealous."

"What?"

"I mean, can I believe — do you believe? — that anybody ever talked this way about me? One week old or any age? Ruining? That somebody wondered?"

"Your mother wondered," Ann Lee says, "whether you knew it or not."

"I doubt it. It was only my father, with her."

"Don't doubt it. I've seen it enough to know. These women who have their babies brought to them when they're still half drugged — they hold their arms out, crane up, they want to see if the baby's all right. That's the first thought, Is he all right, and if not, what can I do? Your mother thought that."

"How do you know?"

She waits, then says, "Because I felt it after I got rid of that one."

He stops his questions, knows better then to prod now.

"They say men in the war feel their legs after they're blown off, always have that ache. I still have that ache, always will — that it's gone, it'll never be here again. But I wonder, too, whether it's all right, as though it got away somewhere, scot-free, but might have impetigo there, or measles . . ."

He says, as softly as he can, "Ann Lee, you'll have another."

"Now that's what I call butting in. Who said you can say that?"

Her humor is thin, sharp. Colby says humbly, "I don't mean necessarily with me. Just you'll arrange it so, some-time — it'll happen, because that's what you want."

"I arranged it so it'll never happen," she says.

It takes a while for that to sink in. "What!? I thought you used rhythm. . . . Why'd you do that?"

"Look, I was already twenty-three, I'd had my time in New York, two years after that on the road, I knew the kind of life I wanted. No more question about that. I wanted to move. I always wanted to move from the time I was stuck as a child. I knew the two things couldn't go together, not for me. Not for me a baby in a rented room, the landlady looking in with a bottle, me running back from rehearsal, hearing him screaming all the way down the street. No. No little child in a crate in a church auditorium, prop girl hovering over him, spooning baby food down with a plastic spoon. No. It can all be done but not by me. No baby without a father, and that's the way it would be — you know that, Col, you're just being silly."

"It's for you. It's what you want."

"That's where you get silly, that's where you and I can't get along. You say like all the others, 'If it makes you happy, do it,' like a baby was a Life Saver, something to pop in your mouth because it's sweet.

"Don't you see, this is something else. This is a question of what I can bring to life, of what I know I can offer, or can't. It's not for fun or even for nourishment, what you silly people call fulfillment — and I'm not making fun of that, either, I told you I still have that ache. It's that first things have to come first, and I know I'll never have a three-bedroom house, a clean bathroom, a washing machine, a five o'clock feeling that somebody's coming home. . . . When we were little, and it was winter, and getting dark around that time, we'd go to the front room window and watch for Daddy's light; he'd be walking home through the woods from the mine, with his lantern. Left before daybreak, came back after nightfall, only saw us in daylight on Sunday. I'm not talking about helping with the housework — he never helped with the housework, how could he? No, I'm talking about somebody else there. The world in pairs. You know the world's in pairs, don't you, Colby? The decent world? You know they never can do away with that?"

"Good Lord," he says, "a speech," because he is overwhelmed by her words, by the dry stare she gives him, the sense that she is beyond him, again, that his childishness is coming on.

"All right, you want me happy," she says, after a while, with a sigh. "You want me happy. I get that."

He wonders whether to take it further, whether now is the time to reach across, take her long hand off the steering wheel, hold it, offer her something. He remembers dreams which stopped when he woke in the middle, thinking, What — ? What birdcall? What words? What message was there, broken off in the middle, lost, the words lost, and also the sleep-sense of power, the thought, Yes, that's it. He does not reach out.

They are driving down to the valley, and he sees the tin-colored cross on the church; they are coming into town, he is on the track now — she has found Pineville, for him.

"Nearly there," she says, glancing at him, gauging his strength. "Is his office in town?"

"Over the hardware store. He should be there."

She reaches out and touches him with the tip of her forefinger, Michelangelo's creating touch, he thinks, sighing, relaxing towards her, longing for a little surcease.

"Don't worry, I'll help you," she says.

They are at the place where the road forks before the gas station. He does not thank her for her offer, appears to ignore it because to accept it raises too many questions.

"Freddy White's branched out," he says, instead. "Look at that used-car lot. Must be five hundred vehicles there. Used to be just a gas station with a few wrecks behind it."

"They've got the road to Cincinnati now, more money, more places to go to spend it. I read where some people work in the city and come home on the weekend, commuting, like New York."

"Money," he says as they ride down Main Street. "Two movie theaters! We never used to have anything but a drive-in, and it didn't matter what they showed, they could have shown nothing, a blank screen, it wouldn't have mattered. We all used to tell each other the plots, beforehand, so when we got home and somebody asked, 'What happened?' we could launch in. Look, there's a Kroger's, I never thought to see a supermarket that size in this town, I guess that means they're living on something more than food stamps. A shoe-repair shop. Now, that is fancy.

"There it is," he adds.

She begins to look for a parking space. The angled-to-the-curb slots the pickups used are gone; the pickups are gone too. There are meters, now, the parking is parallel. Most of the spaces are taken up by foreign-made station wagons and the big dirt-encrusted Pontiacs and Buicks, ten or twelve years old, which used to be rare signs of prosperity.

Ann Lee slides the car into a space, backing and pulling forward smoothly.

Colby gets out and waits for her on the sidewalk. When she doesn't open her door, he leans down to see what she is doing and finds her squinting into the rearview mirror, not applying lipstick, but running a comb through her hair.

Straightening up, he smiles.

Then she steps out daintily and comes to join him. "Where to?"

"I'll show you."

The hardware store has two display windows, which have not been dusted or rearranged in a long time. Last spring's seed packets are lined in rows on a standing rack, the pale green lettuces yellowed from a summer of sun, the radishes blotchy, whitened. "There's moss rose, my mother used to plant it in an old stump, near the house. It has a kind of small rubbery leaf and little bright pink and bright purple flowers. A nothing of a plant," he adds, embarrassed by his own nostalgia.

He dawdles, hooking his thumbs over his waistband. There is a hand cultivator in the window but also, in back, a CB radio and what look like the vital parts to a washing machine. "Herman always was eclectic," he explains.

Ann Lee waits, at his elbow. After a while, she asks, "Do we go through the shop?"

He goes ahead of her around the frame building, sees the saw-toothed brick border his father laid for his cement path. He has also planted shrubs and built a trellis for morning glory vines. The morning glories have not yet been frost-killed; they have reached the top of the fan-shaped trellis and jumped off onto the gutter. Their blue parasols hang limply from the vine; some are scattered on the path at their feet. "Flowers, always flowers," Colby says. "Except for the moss roses, my mother wanted tomatoes and corn."

"Always something to hold against him, Col."

"Well . . ." He opens the door with his father's nameplate on it and is annoyed that Ann Lee hangs back, studying the plate. "That's just his name!"

"I didn't know he was called Jeremiah. Where did the Colby come from?"

"My mother's family. A little more class." He is still holding the door, and she slides through, under his arm, looks up, amused — he is not always a holder of doors. He drops the door handle, flustered. His unease reminds him that he hasn't moved as far as he thought, that the years in Cambridge haven't done for him exactly what he thought they had; he thinks he sees this in her humorous glance, then tries to believe that she has no way of knowing all this. Everything still remains to be said. He follows her up the stairs.

At the top, another door; he looks through the glass panel with its beveled edges catching little rainbows and sees the back of his father's head.

He is sitting at his desk in the small white room with his jacket off and his shirtsleeves rolled up and held by old-fashioned black elastic bands. His head is bowed over the papers on his desk, and Colby sees, beneath the closely cropped gray hair, the groove down the back of his neck. Colby thinks he is studying something legal, a brief, until he sees his father's right hand moving a yellow pencil slowly across the white page.

Without hesitating, Ann Lee knocks, and the head flies up, the body motionless, as though there is no connection. Colby's father looks at him for the first time in twenty-five years out of the corner of his eye.

Ann Lee opens the door.

She is halfway across the patch of bare floor to his father when Colby follows, thinks that he is shuffling and looks at his feet. He is reassured by the look of his loafers, just shined.

Ann Lee is shaking his father by the hand, and his father is looking her over and smiling. Then he turns to Colby; the smile becomes fixed.

"How are you?"

The two men look at each other.

The bristling black eyebrows which Colby remembers have been transformed into white filaments, insectlike, fine and waving: feelers in the place of stingers. The dark eyes underneath have a pert expression as though they are supervising their own decay. The cheeks are lined, gouged, with a smooth patch in the center of each one; the mouth droops a little under the tobacco-stained short gray mustache, which has softened in texture, too. He is wearing as always a white shirt, starched, and Colby knows — it is one of the few details — that since his mother's death, his father has washed, starched and ironed his shirts himself; striped tie, suspenders and iron gray suit pants.

"Looks like you gained weight, Son," his father says. "Looks like five or six pounds."

"In twenty-five years, that's not so bad, is it?" Colby asks and immediately regrets the question.

His father stands up, sliding the chair away abruptly; he pats his own stomach — "Tight as a drum" — and leers at Colby's discomfort. "Any arm wrestling, lately?" the old man asks.

"How's your law practice?"

"Well, you can see I am not exactly overwhelmed with clients."

Ann Lee asks, "What kind of legal trouble do you handle?"

"All kinds," the old man says smoothly, turning his head in a disjointed, mechanical way to study his girl visitor. He is shameless in the way he steps back to get a better look at her legs, then leans forward to follow the line of her thighs under her tight-fitting blue jeans. He is distracted by her jacket, his eyes slide off, he begins to answer her question, laying on as she has laid on his southernness, his creaking courtly charm. "All kinds, young lady, all kinds. Mainly right now disputes with the Scotia Mine Company; there's been a strike, you may have heard of it —"

"Yes, of course I have."

"Well, strikes mean money for lawyers, something this young fellow here never could tolerate; everybody deserves representation," he finishes, rather vaguely.

"You always were a company man," Colby says.

"They deserve representation like anybody else. You all going to sit for a while?"

Colby looks around and does not see a chair aside from the one at the desk. He glances at Ann Lee, who goes and perches herself on the windowsill, looking down at a maze of wires which leads to the hardware store's large sign. "Sit yourself," Colby's father repeats obligingly as he gets down into his chair and wheels it to the desk, facing them.

Colby perches on the other windowsill and finds that his view of Ann Lee is blocked by a filing cabinet, set between the two windows. He cranes forward.

"So, what can I do for you?" his father asks, clapping his hands on his knees.

"We just dropped by. Passing through, on our way to Natural Bridge," Colby explains.

"Well, it's good to see you. Been a long time. You two set up housekeeping in Louisville?"

"Ann Lee's a friend," Colby says stiffly.

"I never did like that first wife of yours. She was thin as the edge of a knife. Nothing good can come out of a woman with no flesh on her bones," he says, appraising Ann Lee, who laughs. "I mean, no kids," the old man explains.

Colby stands up, goes to the desk, peers down at the papers stacked there. He sees short lines in his father's wincing, cautious writing. Short lines spaced evenly down the page. "What's this?"

His father lays one broad hand over the paper. "Just some foolishness."

Colby says, "I remember you reciting, 'They are hangin' Danny Deever, they are marchin' of 'im round . . .'"

"One of the best," his father says, "though Kipling's discredited now." He opens a drawer and pulls out a small pale blue book. "They've got two of mine in here." He hands the book to Colby.

Colby turns to the index, finds his father's name, feels that he cannot face the revelation and hands the book to Ann

Lee. She immediately turns to the selection and bows her head over it. "Oh, good," she says after a moment, as though she has bitten into something sweet.

"I never knew you wrote poetry," Colby says.

"I'd never call it that. Verse. I started after your mother died. I wanted to create an epitaph for her grave. Couldn't find one that didn't seem sickly sweet — you know, the nineteenth-century stonemasons had a book they used for their references. I wanted something strong — couldn't do it, had to turn to Blake. You all won't want to stay here long or I'd take you up to see her."

"Her?" Ann Lee asks.

"Well, I still think of her that way. Her stone looks like her, I mean, even she would be satisfied." He cackles. "Here, have you seen this picture?"

Colby is afraid for a minute that it will be the stone, but when he leans down, he sees a photograph of his mother in a gilt frame on the desk. She looks unimaginably young, under the glass, her skin smoothed out, her hair in a neat bundle at the back of her head, her eyes glazed and bright as beads. "Who in the world took that?" Colby says in an attempt to express his intolerance.

"That was the year before we got married," his father says, holding the photograph out to Ann Lee.

"It doesn't look like her," Colby complains.

"It's not supposed to," his father says. Then he appeals to Ann Lee. "Would you say a photograph of a dead person is supposed to be the spitting image?"

Ann Lee considers. "I guess you could say it is supposed to be better than that."

"That's the consolation!" Colby's father says. "You'll want to know if I miss her," he adds, turning to Colby, "since you haven't been near me since she died —"

"The reason —"

"The answer is, no — not in the day-to-day way. You know, I always have been pretty self-sufficient. My routine goes on pretty much the same. What I miss is the expression on her face — I see it flash by sometimes when I make some remark to myself, that My Gawd look she always had, even when she was dying, as though she never heard tell or expected to hear tell of anything like life. Well, she was shockable," he says gently, to Ann Lee, "and I guess I came to depend on shocking her."

Colby says, "She never did learn how to handle you. That's what I find so hard to forgive her, and you are supposed to forgive the dead everything."

His father stares at him. "Handle me!"

Ann Lee says swiftly, "Did you two ever fight?"

Now both men are looking at her. "You mean me and my wife?" Colby's father asks.

"No, I mean you two."

Colby sees his father begin to puff up as he leans over the desk, fixing her with sharp brown eyes. "We used to arm-wrestle quite a lot," he says.

Colby says, "We did."

"Never would keep himself in shape," his father explains to Ann Lee. "Bright as they come, but never would do anything about the machinery."

He is rolling his sleeve up and positioning his elbow on the desk.

"I am not going to arm-wrestle you," Colby says.

Ann Lee comes off her perch on the windowsill. "Will you let me try?" she asks.

Colby's father is delighted; he chuckles, gives his sleeve an extra roll. His bare white arm, almost hairless, looks as slender as a child's, but Colby knows that is deceptive. "Be careful, Ann Lee, he broke my mother's arm once."

"That was flipping," his father says. "I don't flip no more." It is his first grammatical mistake, and Colby sets it down for proof that, this once, he is not lying.

Still he is afraid for Ann Lee. He goes to stand beside her as she leans over the desk, rolling up the thick sleeve of her white sweater. Her forearm remains honey brown from the summer, thick with soft blond hair. As she plants her elbow on the desktop, his father grasps her small hand.

He begins to press her down slowly, not hurrying, grinning all the time. Ann Lee holds her ground.

After a while, Colby sees Ann Lee grimace and also sees her hand lower an inch towards the desk. "Let up, now," he tells her. "You've held him off a long time already."

And it flashes through his mind — the image of his mother skittering like a paper cutout across the kitchen, weightless, airy, moving in a slow arc towards the wall.

"Let up, now, Ann Lee, there's no use —"

She goes on striving.

"My God," Colby says, after a minute. "Can't you let him win?"

He does not dare to speak to his father. That grin has silenced him.

Ann Lee's hand slams down on the desk. His father lets

go, jumps up, crying, "Honey, you all right?" Ann Lee is nursing her forearm. "You are strong!" he cries.

"Now, Col," his father says firmly, making a gesture as though he is going, one more time, to unbuckle his belt and pull it out of his pants. "Now, Col, your turn!"

Colby leans down over the desk and places his elbow. He does not bother to roll up his shirtsleeve. He is listening for the whine of that belt in the air, swearing to himself not to cry, never to cry, never to give his father that satisfaction.

And remembering his own white buttocks, reflecting in the mirror on the back of the bathroom door: the delirium of his helplessness, his cock leaping.

He snatches at his father's hand, grazes it with his nails, leans down, puffing. As soon as his father clasps his fingers and begins to apply his steady pressure, down, down, always down, Colby knows he has no chance. He struggles, pants, pushes up from underneath, but already he is on the way down and his hand crashes onto the surface of the desk.

"Goddamn," Colby says, smelling his own sweat.

His father is already rolling down his sleeve. "I used to play that game with your mother," he says. "Honey, you all right?" he asks Ann Lee again.

She, too, is rolling down her sleeve. "Yes, all right."

"I believe you held out longer than old Colby here!"

"My God," Colby says, "is it never going to end?"

His father says so monotonously that Colby is not certain he is hearing him right, "It was all games with your mother, don't you know, all games. Let your girlfriend here tell you, women like it sometimes, it helps them sometimes, kind of interrupts their problems."

Colby says, "I don't know what you're talking about."

"Then listen," Ann Lee says, returning to her perch.

Colby strides to the window, looks down at the street, sees two men on the other side going into the Mountainview Cafeteria, sees the philodendrons in the window, the curled signs from last spring's cake sales. Let me not hear, this one time, he thinks. If he wants to talk, let him talk, but let me not hear.

"Yes," his father is saying in a voice which is ripe with the weight of the words; he is studying Ann Lee, directing it all at her with the shavings and splinters left over for Colby. "You, a young girl, wouldn't know what I mean —"

"Not so young."

"Listen, she was a woman — Colby's mother — oh, quite some woman, taught school when I met her, could keep those twelve-year-olds in line like nobody's business. I mean she had the backbone, then, the nerve, in a little lean body that was never much more than a child's." He smacks his lips in appreciation and Colby winces. "She had trouble letting go of herself and we found these ways. Play-fighting. You know what play-fighting is — childish, maybe, but it helped."

Ann Lee says, "Yes," and Colby wants to strike her. Why yes? What does she know?

"I mean, I would take her by the arm, like this, when she was being cranky," and he actually gets up from his desk and goes over to the window and takes hold of Ann Lee's arm, just above the elbow, "I would take hold of her arm and kind of twist her, nothing much, you know, kind of a twist to give her a taste of her own strength. She didn't weigh but one hundred and eleven pounds, but she was quite strong." And he twists. Ann Lee with a shudder turns and is facing out instead of facing the old man, as though she has turned as naturally and smoothly as the earth turning around the sun; she is moving around Colby's father, with her whisper of protest or compliance, smoothly, her sneakers running along under the cuffs of her blue jeans. All the way around him.

"Stop that," Colby says.

Ann Lee has come back to her original place and is staring at Colby's father, who is smiling as though he is about to give her a special prize. "Pretty good," he says, and then, "I used to flip her —"

"No!" Colby steps forward. As he approaches his father, he smells the rank sweated wool of his father's dark suit pants, which he has been living in for twenty years, inspecting the seams for cracks, letting his own sour sweat build up in the material. "Let go of her," he says to his father, and begins to pry his fingers off Ann Lee's arm, one at a time, but as he pries each finger up and goes on to the next, the last finger closes on her arm again. It does not seem that Ann Lee is helping him any, and Colby peers at her face and sees that she is staring at his father. "Oh, stop that," he says — she looks like a rabbit in the glare of a headlight, caught in the middle of the road. "Oh, can't you stop that." His father's wide horny hand is stopping her; he has caught her as Colby once saw him catch a chicken by the wing and the leg, swing it against the shed wall, bash out its brains, "Easier and quicker than wringing its neck."

"Let go of her," Colby shouts, using a voice he didn't know he had. He catches hold of Ann Lee by the shoulders and wrenches her backwards. Not until Ann Lee raises her held arm does the old man's hand slide off. Ann Lee is let go.

"Now why you want to do that?" Colby's father asks him, aggrieved.

"We're leaving," Colby shouts, "we're leaving — why we ever came —"

"To see me?" the old man asks. "Was that why?"

Colby has Ann Lee under her arm; he crushes up the sag of her sweater in his hand, half-lifts her towards the door, her feet are dangling like the cardboard feet on the two-eared balloons his father used to buy him at Fountain Ferry. She is scraping along, weightless, protesting, but not too much. "Let's go," Colby says, and he hurries her through the door, realizing now that they are the only trade to have passed through that door in months; that the pile of papers on his father's desk is poetry or catalogs; that there is no secretary, no telephone, no typewriter; that his father is an old man, at last, alone in an empty room over a hardware store and that he, Colby, is proof against it.

"Good-bye," he shouts from the bottom of the stairs because he knows his father is standing at the top, listening, keeping his head drawn back out of sight. Colby slams the door.

Ann Lee, floating in his grip, sighs.

"Don't sigh at me," he mutters, looking for a way to shove her, fast, into his car.

"Colby, you are crazy," she says, and he imagines or hopes to hear some admiration. "Your father was just trying to play with me."

"Play with you!" He takes his hand, his free-floating

broad-backed white hand, and hits her across the side of the face, hearing the satisfying wallop as the air in her cheek gushes out, watching the way the shape of his palm appears on her cheek, in scorched red, watching the way she feels the place with the tips of her fingers and gazes at him as though she has never seen him before. "You won't let anybody touch you, to love you — why him? Why him?"

"He's an old man," she says, wiping the tears out of her eyes, and he watches her feeling that red place and knows that he has impressed her finally, that words would never have done this, could never have done this, and that this is the lesson his father learned, throwing the shadow body of his wife against the wall.

"I'm not getting in that car with you," she says, sounding frightened.

"The hell you're not." But he weakens, watching her, and she takes advantage of the moment to step off the sidewalk, into the street, still holding her blazing cheek with her left hand; and hold out her right, thumb up.

"You're not getting out of here that way," he shouts at her, then doubles over, laughing into his knees, because she is standing there by the line of parked cars, in the middle of the main street in Pineville, trying to hitch a ride.

People are passing behind him along the sidewalk, and he feels their stares loading him down as he steps between two cars. "You're never going to get out of here that way!" he shouts.

She waits for a little, tentatively, then folds her thumb in and goes towards his car. It is locked. He stands watching her, then walks over and unlocks his side of the car and climbs in. He slams the door, watching her through the windshield. It is as though he is signing an agreement with her, silently, through the glass. He starts the motor, inches the car towards her until she is right against the bumper; he knows that she will not move, that she will let him run her down before she will move. He nudges her knees with the bumper, foot cautious on the brake, a nudge, nothing else, and hears someone on the sidewalk shout. Then he reaches over and flips up the lock and she gets in.

"I could have run you over, you know that?" he asks cheerfully. "I could have run you over."

"That's why I got in the car. I'm riding with you back to Louisville."

"Excuse me, Natural Bridge," he says. "We are going to Natural Bridge for the weekend."

For a moment she is silent. Then she says, into the windshield, "All right, I'll go with you."

"You don't have any choice!"

"Oh yes, I do," she says, and this time she turns to stare at him and he sees the flicker of fear in her eyes fade out. "I always have a choice."

"Big words," Colby says. "Big words!" But he loves her determination to take the risk — any risk. It must have loomed at her in many shapes and forms on highways and at rest stops and one-night motels, and she must always have said, Yes. I choose it. I will always choose.

But this time, it's different. "You're never going to know what I may do next," he says, pressing down the accelerator. "I'm not like those other ones" — and he wants, suddenly, to brag about something, his intelligence — but doesn't quite dare. Maybe it doesn't matter, in the end.

She does not speak to him again. She sits with her hands

flat on her knees, her feet planted on the floor, and Colby begins to laugh, he beats his hands against the steering wheel, guffawing, knows that nothing she can give him and nothing she can withhold will matter, now, that he has her, that he will always have her, as long as he can reach over and grab her, kiss her, lift her off her feet — what does it matter? She weighs about a hundred pounds.

16

"YOU MIGHT LIKE the chicken," he is saying, two hours later, in the sunset-colored dining room at the Natural Bridge lodge. The waitress has seated them next to a large fieldstone column which supports not the ceiling but a nest of high-flying philodendrons and fireplace plants. The dark green leaves dip down over their heads. Outside the plate glass windows, the sun is setting in a bloodbath over the preserved forest.

"The chicken here is good, not greasy," he goes on when she does not reply.

She looks at him for the first time, steadily. "What about the corn bread?"

"Bound to be good."

He orders. His voice has never sounded so clipped. He feels that he is impressing the room, making a mark on the air.

The chicken comes after their long silence. She tucks the end of her napkin into her neck, obedient as a frightened child.

"You can pick it up," he says when she raises her fork.

"I don't want to."

"Even my aunt," he begins, then gives up the attempt. He picks up a heavy piece of chicken, a thigh, perhaps, and begins to gnaw on it.

"At least keep hold of your table manners," she says with a subdued twinkle.

"I'll do that." He puts his chicken back down on the plate and attacks it with knife and fork. "After supper, we'll go out for a walk —"

"It'll be dark. It'll be cold."

"Maybe not. The sun's not down, yet. I'd like to take you up onto the bridge. I've never been there before. We didn't do much sightseeing when I was growing up. Waste of time."

"Me neither. We went once to Chimney Rock in North Carolina. Dad fussed all the way back because it cost a quarter apiece, and he said the view was the same he could see from his own back porch . . ."

He appreciates her ordinary talk. Reaching across the table he pats the back of her hand and sees her wince away. He is shocked. "Don't do that, honey. Don't do that." He remembers a child in school who always pulled back like that from the teacher, always expecting a blow.

"I want to get back to town tomorrow, I have a tech rehearsal," she says. "Eleven o'clock."

"We'll get an early start."

"Is that a promise?"

"That's a promise."

She goes on eating her chicken, then proceeds methodically to the corn bread, crumbles off a bit, tastes it.

"Are you enjoying yourself?" he asks.

She stares at him. He flushes, drops his eyes.

From then on it is silence. Finally they get up from the table, stuffed, gorged, like the other couples in the room who are drifting off towards the cigarette machine (there is no bar, the county is dry), shuffling downstairs to the men's room, adjusting belt buckles, settling into overstuffed chairs. To Colby, the thick warm air seems stirred by anticipation, wafted with the heat from vent to vent — something, anything must happen to justify the weekend, the outlay of money and time and energy, the gasoline, the hope, the drive . . . Something. Anything.

"Do you want your coat? It'll be cool up there," he says.

"I didn't bring one. Martha needed hers back. The tan jacket is all I have." Absentminded, she slips it on.

"You should have borrowed a coat from somebody in the company."

"The only one I liked was going to the Breaks of Sandy."

He smiles, delighted by her reviving humor, hoping it will save them. "Come on, let's get started."

They stroll out onto the porch, suddenly hand in hand. How the others must envy them, imagining that something, anything can still happen between them. They stroll down the long steps to a mast of signs: BRIDGE TRAIL, CAVE, THREE-MILE HIKE, DRINKING FOUNTAIN. It is still light enough to make out the words. Colby starts off on Bridge Trail.

He feels her hesitate, at the end of his arm, feels the fluttering backward motion he remembers from fishing, that moment before the hook is set. "Come on." She follows.

They start up the dusty winding path, worn deeply by the

summer's traffic. The edges are set with limestone splinters and the draggled clay roots of ferns. The ferns themselves, dusty and bowed, stretch away under the dark pines. The trash cans are tree trunks, the benches are logs supported on other logs, akilter, as though about to roll away.

"We used to talk about coming here every Fourth of July," Colby says. "Never made it." He rubs her warm pliable hand. The path is narrow. He must drop her hand almost at once and relinquish her, allowing her to follow behind.

"We came once," she says. "It was my brother's birthday, my littlest brother, he was seven, he said nothing was ever done for his birthday, which was true. Who has time for that kind of thing? He must have hit a raw spot — Daddy always said we had the best raising lack of money could supply — because we were all piled in the car, next thing, and driven up here. Fall, about this time, I remember the chilled smell. Then it turned out there was no room in the inn for us — all six of us — though Dad would have crammed us into two double beds, family beds, they called them. No, they didn't even have one room or didn't like the look of us, I don't know which. So we went back home. Got there around suppertime. I remember we ate early, on the road. First meal away from home I remember; I was nine. Ate catfish in some diner, and my brother was pleased, said that was the way a birthday ought to be."

She stops and draws breath as though she is tired.

They are climbing, now, the path grows steep, worn by feet down to the rock ledges. Colby reaches back to help her along but she avoids his hand, leaping nimbly from ledge to ledge, and he is reminded of a vase painting of Orpheus leading Eurydice, reaching blindly back for her hand. Colby has no intention of looking back. Besides, it is getting dark.

They come out in a clearing at the top of the hill and look down at the lodge, a nest of lights. A chill wind is blowing. Ann Lee wraps her jacket around her.

"You're cold," Colby says.

"Yes."

He hesitates to commiserate, says instead, "How's your play going?"

"My —?" She stops there. "It's going pretty well. My two sisters are pretty much what you would expect — local talent, a little spoiled, each one a star in her church group. They have a lousy male lead — for once, you'd agree. He's from Cincinnati."

"How's Grant Tom?"

"Fine, except he says you are never to darken the door. Your actor — the one you threw off the stage —"

"Let down off the stage is more like it."

"Whichever. I'm not going to argue with you, Colby. Anyway, his family gave ten thousand dollars when the Ten-Cent was trying to get started — there's a plaque near the front door."

"Grant Tom pays attention to that."

"Grant Tom has to pay attention to that. He quieted the guy down, but it took some doing."

"I couldn't stand the way he was with you."

"He was nothing with me."

"That's not what I saw."

"He's gay, Colby." She laughs. "Am I supposed to be flattered? You're jealous so easily?"

"You are supposed to be whatever you are." He is uneasy, seeing for the first time her bent towards him, the slip in her independence, seeing it as a twist of her character like the twist of an oar blade, seen through water.

Trying to remember that she is not his, will never be his, he lets her pass ahead of him on the narrow path. She walks rapidly. He watches her neat sharp strides: she is taking on the ascent, in her methodical directed way, as she took on the part, the lines, her life in a new town. Methodical, quick, not easy. He allows the distance between them to widen, playing with the idea of abandoning her, playing with the idea of his own objectivity. She'll be gone anyway, he thinks, in a matter of weeks.

She passes ahead of him out of the clearing, and he realizes that he is allowing her to go alone onto the bridge. This is the moment he has imagined them sharing.

Still he does not hurry.

Coming along slowly behind, he sees her standing in the failing light on the center of the heavy stone arch. Its thrust forces the walls of the valley apart. The bridge is broad, worn smooth, pale gray in the draining light, a sidewalk with the sadness of a manmade thing, useful, without innocence.

Ann Lee stands in the middle of it. Colby halts at an edge. He imagines himself crouching, an Indian with bent bow, advancing inch by inch on his prey.

Ann Lee raises her head, looks up at the sky, where the first colorless stars are pricking, then down into the valley, where the lights of the new road twine. She puts her hands on her hips, bends low, then straightens up, leans back until Colby imagines her backbone straining. He stands still, watching. In hotel rooms all over the Midwest, she will one day be practicing her stretching. On the knobby tweed carpets in old downtown rookeries from Kentucky to Kansas and south to the Gulf. There will be things happening along the way — plays, men — but what will matter will be the repetition of her gestures, of her words, of her exercises, alone. He knows now that she is encased in her routine, that her shadowiness is less real than assumed, that she will stroll down the states as the boy hero whose stories he grew up on strolled down the hills between sheep-eating monsters, three-headed giants. "Who goes there?" "Nobody but Jack." She has mastered her needs.

He walks out onto the bridge. "How do you like it?" he asks, touching her shoulder.

She is coming up out of a forward bend. "It's too dark to admire the view."

"What are you doing, exercises?"

"I felt the need to stretch."

He puts his arm lightly around her waist. "You know, I was just thinking of the back of my father's head."

"When we first went in his office?"

"Yes."

She does not say anything.

"Ann Lee, don't you think we might . . ."

She turns to look at him. "Don't ask, Col."

"I don't want to ask."

"Then don't." She waits. The lengthening silence slices them apart. Colby feels the loss of possibilities. He feels the loss of hope. How specific those losses have become — the future picked off in incidents, like sparrows on a wire.

"Let's go back down." She turns.

He has expected more than this out of the bridge. Now he begins to make a list of his disappointments: birthdays, failed screaming Christmases, all the bad anniversaries of his life. Nothing to mark and so nothing except bad temper. Honesty in that if in nothing else. He remembers his wife, on their first anniversary, working late grading papers, looking up out of the circle of light at her desk: Yes, Col? What, Col? Oh, is it really, Col? And he gave her a glass of champagne.

To celebrate what? The mere fact of survival? Is that enough, to celebrate?

He follows Ann Lee back down the path, back down into the valley, to the lodge. It's dark, the path is rough, and he grabs her hand.

Coming into the lobby, they both blink.

"You want something to drink?" he asks.

"It's dry."

"I mean coffee or something."

"Not particularly."

He takes the key from the man at the desk and leads her down the long padded corridor where canned music is playing.

Inside their room, he switches on a metal lamp. The rest of the room is dark, swathed in heavy curtains, dumpy bedspreads. Ann Lee begins right away to take off her clothes, standing in the middle of the floor, dragging things off over her head and dropping them.

"Aren't you going to —" Awkwardly, he gestures at the bathroom.

"You don't want to see me undress?"

When he does not answer, she continues, unbuttoning her denim shirt, releasing the luxuriance of her breasts.

He must go to her. The lack of ceremony must be forgotten.

He sobs as he touches her. What was elaborate is made simple as he feels her nipples straighten under his fingers. He reaches inside the waistband of her jeans, feeling for her belly, for the quiver he will find there. Her body is still calm and warm, water which cannot be ruffled. He begins to stroke her cunt, willing her wetness. She does not move, does not change, he feels her integral resistance, her endless emotional chastity.

He pushes her down onto the bed. His father's voice comes back to him, a stormy mumbling of warnings, advice: interrupt their problems. That's it. Resistance is clothed in passive flesh. He unbuttons his pants, takes out his stiff penis. He throws her over onto her stomach, pulls her jeans down, spreads her a little, rams in. There is no wetness, no response. He comes in two pushes.

Then he is lying still on top of her.

"Why did you let me?"

"Let?" Her voice is buried in her arm.

"Why did you — ?"

"You do what you want, Colby."

He rolls off her. There are tears on his cheeks.

Going into the bathroom, he turns on the fierce spluttering blue light and looks at his face in the mirror, feels along his jaws with his fingers, wonders if he will hurt her, if he has already hurt her, if he will have the privilege and the pleasure of hurting her again.

Back in the bedroom, he sees her still lying that way and jerks the sheet up over her.

Then he takes off his clothes in the dark and lies down beside her. There will be no cuddling, no warmth. They will lie side by side, waiting for the light. He decides not to sleep. She will not sleep. She has not moved since he came.

He remembers the game of statues and feels that he has thrown her into her final pose, lying on her stomach on the bed. He stares into the darkness, which separates in front of his eyes, becoming gray particles, shifting, as though the darkness is a storm of molecules. He wants to hear her breathe. He can hear nothing.

He is surprised when he feels himself falling asleep finally, next to her woodenness, and his surprise pursues him down into the deep underwater trench where he dreams they are dancing together, in sunshine.

17

COLDNESS CREEPING: he shifts. The sheet and the thin hotel blanket are crumpled, and with one hand he smooths them out. Tucks the edges of the cover under his arm, holds the warmth in. Night turning cold outside the curtained window: the dull silence of the stuffy building. Somebody rolling a service cart down the padded hall. Still the cold moves along, under the covers now, sliding up his side, across his shoulders. He hunches down, turns slightly, pushes his hand out along the bed. His hand skids across the sheet, out into the cold; he jerks wide awake, sits up in bed, throws the thin covers back.

"Ann Lee?"

His voice is muffled. Then he sits and waits. He does not want to get up and look in the bathroom; there is no light under the door. Finally he has no choice. He gets up, opens the bathroom door, switches on the glaring light.

For a while, he stands staring at the fixtures, at the glasses in their plastic sleeves, the soap wrapped in printed paper; nothing has been used, even the towels hang in their original folds. He wonders if she has been in this antiseptic space, peers into the sink as though expecting to find a hair. There is nothing. She has not even taken a drink. He goes back into the bedroom.

"Ann Lee . . ."

He feels that he is bleating into the darkness and, with his hand, he closes his mouth.

Now he must begin to think. It is not enough to stand around, staring, listening, waiting. He must plan what to do next.

He realizes that he is naked and begins to scrape together his clothes from the floor, in the dark; finally thinks to turn on the light and then is forced to see that there is no scrap of hers left in the room. She has pulled herself together, dressed herself, taken everything, even the change she put in the ash-tray.

He pulls on his shorts, his pants, sits down on the bed to put on his socks. The musty smell of the bed reminds him that they were together there once, but already that is fiction, long passed out of mind. He has always known that she will go, has known it from the first time he saw her, on the thruway with the Coke in her hand.

But she has no money. He has seen her wallet, knows that she has a couple of dollars, some change. How will she manage?

That has never stopped her, but it lends a legitimacy to his worry, that he must provide her with transportation to wherever it is she wants to go, that he must see to it that she has a meal before she starts out. A coat, even. She has gone out into the darkness with no coat.

He snatches up his jacket, thrusts his belongings into the blue plastic bag which he threw on a chair the night before.

Then he opens the door and launches out into the glaring corridor.

At the desk in the lobby, a small man is leaning over a newspaper as though inspecting it for a flaw. Colby rams his hand onto the counter to get his attention, does not apologize for the startle. The man puts the bill together, shuffles endlessly with figures, sighs. Meanwhile, Colby is trying to decide to ask him whether or not he has seen Ann Lee.

"A young woman . . . girl . . ."

The man does not lift his head.

"Leaving . . ."

He cannot phrase it as a question, so the man simply ignores him. As he slides the bill across the counter, he asks, "You say something?"

"No," Colby says. He does not want the clerk to lay a finger on her, even with words.

Having paid, he goes out into the heavy dark. There are no stars, no moon. There is no creak of sound. One window, on the top floor, is lighted and seems to give off a semblance of hope: someone is up there, awake, and for a moment, Colby imagines that she is there, having decamped to another room.

He goes to the parking lot, feeling for his keys. After a little, he searches the other pocket, then stops to consider. He is methodical, and his keys are always in the same place, the right-hand pocket of his pants, but he suddenly wonders whether, this one time, he took them out and left them on the dresser in the room. He knows he did not. There was no time for that. He stands in the middle of the parking lot, surrounded by the humped shapes of cars. Then he walks slowly to the retaining wall where he parked, the evening before. He remembers choosing the place because the wall cast a shadow which seemed snug for the car. The space is empty.

He knows that already. It is not a surprise. Still he stands and stares.

Then he smiles, laughs once. He has to admire her nerve.

After that, he begins to think of the problem — the fact that he is for the first time in his adult life stranded, with no means of transportation. There is no car rental service at the lodge, no bus, airplane or train. He is simply stranded until daybreak, when he perhaps can hitch to Lexington and rent a car.

He imagines his father, in the office in Pineville, listening to his story.

He turns back to the lodge. Inside, he approaches the clerk, vastly humbled, and asks for the further use of his room. The clerk is apparently used to quixotic behavior, for he sighs and hands back the key. Colby explains that he will be leaving as planned in the morning. He cannot bear to confess to the clerk that his car is gone.

Then he has to face going back into the room. He knows the way its smell and silence will accost him; knows that he will never be able to sleep in that bed. He imagines Ann Lee following the threads of his headlights down the mountains. All this time, he is standing outside the door to the room, the key in his hand.

All right. He veers aside, shifts the weight of his plastic satchel. Better the lobby.

He goes quietly past the clerk, who does not seem to be interested, finds a deep chair near the fieldstone fireplace, sits down opposite a bucket of plants. The leaves, leaping out of the bucket, are hard and green, and he understands why this plant is so well-equipped to survive. An enormous orange-shaded lamp on the table by his left arm is flooding him with its unsettling light; after a moment, he creeps his hand across and switches the light off and then waits, stiff in the back of the neck, for the clerk across the lobby to protest. He does not protest. Colby leans back his head and closes his dry eyes.

Was it the fucking? She didn't like —

Didn't like!

Didn't like that he had a hold —

That for the first time she was doing something that was not right for her.

That she was —

Subdued subjected broken

No!

Not Ann Lee.

Then what?

The memory of her half-naked body sprawled on the bed is hideous to him. He knows that he never meant to reduce her to that and knows at the same time that this is irrelevant. He remembers atrocious murders, pleas of insanity, all the garbage of the rational mind. The fact is he did it. They did it, together. She would accept her responsibility for it, too. They did it. She must find that the hardest to bear, she who based her pride on her sure unfailing instinct for self-preservation, who once laughed when he talked about suffering women, mistreated women, women as victims: "Not me, Col . . ."

Yet she lay there.

He dozes a little. The lighted lobby rocks in front of his eyes when he opens them. There is no sound, no change in the density of the air, still a long way from morning.

He begins to think of the things that make pain almost bearable: a cup of good coffee, a clean shirt, the feel and the smell of a new hardcover book, ordered, waited for, gratefully received. He knows that if he was in his own place, he would find this pain less overwhelming; he would begin his routines, cook something, rearrange something, gather his feathers around him. Here he is bare.

He dozes, again, then jerks up, hoping that hours have passed. The light is the same in the lobby, the air is the same. How can the night go on and on? It is only 4:00 A.M., only an hour since he woke up and found her gone.

Sleep, you fool, he lectures himself, then knows it is no use, sits up, rubs his eyes, begins to leaf through the magazines on the table, all out-of-date hunting and fishing guides. He remembers packing a change of clothes and thinking, No book this time. No need.

He leafs through advertisements for rowboats, cabin cruisers, fishing tackle of all kinds, wonders why this part of the man's world never appealed to him. His mind wanders, he dozes, drops his head back on the end of his stiff neck, winces. Then a deeper sleep sets in. Its currents whirl him. He is dreaming of a calm beyond all this, a patch in the woods at home where he built a stick lean-to, his first adventure alone; the first time he realized he could walk far enough from the house to be out of range of his mother's call. Seven, maybe eight. The first freedom. Then at once the attempt to build — the stick lean-to in the woods.

He jerks up in the chair. Someone is talking near him. The lobby is full of strained morning light.

He gets to his feet stiffly, wants to raise his hands, praise God for the fact that the night is gone. He stares around. There are people near him, in clusters and alone, coming from the dining room. A man in the next chair is reading the morning paper.

Now he will have to begin to arrange his escape. First he goes into the men's room, washes his bleary face, sees that he needs a shave, urinates with relief. He washes his hands, smooths out the wrinkles in his shirt, tries to find a look of competence, energy. He will have to persuade someone to do something for him, to get him out. He goes back to the lobby.

First, though, breakfast. He is aware of an incredibly fierce hunger and knows that he must stock himself for the escape.

The dining room is full of light, tepee napkins, waitresses in pink smocks. He is ushered to a small table which barely covers his knees. The menu offers buckwheat cakes. He smiles at the suggestion and starts a dimple in the face of the skinny mountain girl who is waiting for his order. "Now don't bring me that four-percent maple syrup," he warns her, and she promises, giggling, to bring him some of the heavy black molasses he remembers. As she scurries off, he spreads his napkin over his knees, imagines becoming the kind of character who speaks of collard greens and fatback with affection.

The girl arrives with his cakes and something dark-looking in a bottle; it has no label and he sniffs it suspiciously.

Yes, the right thing.

Interested, she hovers nearby, a sparrow of a girl in a flashing pink smock. It stands out from her thin body, seems a shield in itself. He tells her that he is from the city and she seems absurdly impressed. "Stranded here," he says jocosely, "no way to get back." She gapes. Stranded? He does not need to explain to her how or why, she is caught on the word itself, on the bare thought.

Well now she has a brother five miles down the road, married, three children already (Colby listens patiently) was working in the mines till this last layoff . . . a pickup . . . no telephone in the house but the neighbor . . .

He smiles. It is despair, he thinks, which makes everything easy.

"As long as he will let me pay."

She looks at him, wrinkles her nose as though she has smelled something foul. "You can fix that up with him, Mister." Now there is space between them, to his relief. She goes off to telephone.

He is dawdling over his last bite when she comes back to announce that the neighbor was at home and willing to carry the message. A chain of events is started and Colby realizes that he will simply be carried along. He prods the bit of pancake with his fork, swipes it through the syrup, invites the girl to sit down and have a cup of coffee; she refuses but hovers with the hot scorched-smelling electric percolator, filling his cup again and again. Then she goes away and he sees her gulping three of four mouthfuls of water, bent over the fountain, one hand holding her short uniform down behind.

Later she announces that the pickup has arrived as though

she invented the machine. Colby goes to the front door. There it is, blue, mud-caked, its owner standing by with arms folded. One glance at the chapped, red-bearded face and Colby suspects that he will not be asking about money. The girl touches her brother's arm, goes about making an introduction which the young man ignores with a flip of his chin. "Hop in."

Colby hops. He leans out of the window to tell the girl goodbye, to thank her, sees that she has already turned away.

"Where to?" the driver asks, shifting gears with an ominous wrench and rattle under the floor. The glove compartment falls open, belching a dirty rag. There is a cavity on the dashboard where a CB radio is fastened, sprouting insectlike antennas. "Down the hill, anywhere you want," Colby says, having failed to arm himself with a plan.

"I'll take you to Lexington, you can get a bus there," the young man says firmly. It is apparent to Colby that he has helped his sister before, not unwilling but inside of certain set limits.

They begin the long descent into the valley. It is early morning; the sun behind the tall tulip poplars casts grids of light across the road. The coal trucks, already loaded, labor up hills in front of them, gather speed, hurtle past on the downslope. Colby's driver plays hopscotch with them, passing grandly on the upgrade, pumping the accelerator furiously to keep ahead of them, going down. Sometimes he succeeds in staying ahead with the black monster panting behind him: Colby looks back once or twice to see the long outside mirrors on the coal truck flashing like a pair of appraising eyes. Other times, the truck with a maniacal horn blast passes the pickup, swerving out around turns. It appears that Bobby knows most of the drivers; he claps the outside of his door with one hand and bellows when they pass him.

In between, he tells Colby about his farm in a hollow nearby; they raise some vegetables, a little corn, but the only money comes from his job in the mine. He is out of work because of another wildcat strike and he grins and shakes his head over it as though it is a misbehaving infant, annoying yet to be admired for its temerity.

"You do something, down there?" he asks Colby after a long silence.

"I teach."

"You teach in Louisville?" He pronounces the name the way foreigners do, with all its syllables intact.

"Yes, in the university there."

"They pay much? Excuse me," Bobby adds.

"I can live," Colby says stiffly, realizing that he has been outflanked. He lays his hands out on his knees, then cannot resist the comparison to the horny claws on the steering wheel.

They leave the thruway and swoop down into Lexington, bouncing suddenly over potholes, in the ghetto, and Bobby flaps his hand at the scene, but to Colby, it is peaceful, nearly pastoral. The frame shotgun houses are all painted white. He does not see anything shameful about this world.

"Here you are," Bobby says abruptly, stopping the truck in front of the Greyhound station. "So long," he says with his first grin, which reveals a good many large teeth; he sticks out his hand. Colby takes it, feels the wide ridges in the well-worked skin. "Good-bye." Bobby is off before Colby can think of money.

Colby goes into the bus station, finds that there is a bus for Louisville in twenty minutes. He buys himself a ticket, briefly wondering that she did not palm his wallet; then he goes to the pay phone.

It is a long time before the telephone is answered. He lets it go on ringing, imagining Martha nursing the baby, finally getting up and going downstairs.

She does answer in the end.

"Ann Lee come back yet?" Colby asks.

"Come back! I thought she was with you!"

"She was, but she left sometime in the night. I thought she might have made it home."

There is a pause. "No," Martha says. Then she asks, "You all right?"

"No," Colby says. "I'm in Lexington, I'm going to catch a bus."

"When will you be here?"

"About two hours."

"All right," she says. "I'll call I., we'll meet you at the station."

That is all Colby needs to hear. The car, and Martha and I. He hangs up. It seems that again he is going to be helped. He goes into the cafeteria and orders himself a cup of coffee. He doctors it with sugar and dehydrated milk, which makes a mosaic of dissolving particles on the surface. As he stirs the mosaic in, he realizes that he is very cold.

It is a mild autumn morning, sun is straining through the dirty windows, the letters of the cafeteria's name are repro-

duced in reversed shadows on the checked floor. But he is
cold. He is very cold. He rubs his hands together, stamps his
feet.

"You all right, Mister?" It is another woman, this one a
nurse of some kind, her white oblong cap pinned on top of
a mighty bun.

"Just cold."

"I got the heat up as high as it will go."

"This coffee will help," he says, and sips.

The nurse goes away. Colby looks out the window and
sees the bus wallowing into the parking lot. He jumps up.
The nurse makes him sit while she transfers the coffee into a
carrying container with a top. "Plenty of time, plenty of
time," she says. Then she takes a long time making change
out of his last five-dollar bill. His is hopping with anxiety, his
eyes fixed on the bus's open door; the driver is lolling alongside, two passengers have climbed in. He rushes out, at last,
his satchel bouncing against his knees. "What's the hurry?"
the driver asks him as he takes his ticket. "We got another
eleven minutes."

Colby hunches forward as they hurtle down through the
Bluegrass. The six-lane highway is brand-new, sleekly gray
and empty. It runs through a series of horse farms, cuts
through rolling limestone-fed pastures, snaking white
fences. Here and there clusters of horses are arranged on the
pale wintry green.

"All right," Colby says to himself. "All right. She is bound
to be there." He will not let himself see any further than the
meeting with the Weeklys.

One of the other passengers, a long-legged, scarecrow

man, stretches himself out across the bus's rear seat; his arms dangle, he begins to snore. Colby turns to gawk in admiration, then feels lassitude pass like a blessing; he leans back against the high back of his seat, tilted his chin up, assumes a serious position. He is asleep in no time although dignity prevents him from sprawling. He does not snore.

The dream is of a long path along the river. The path is edged with wild oats, chicory and dock. Colby is walking along the path, parting the overhanging weeds with his hands, towards an open space where he knows he will be able to see the water. Reaching the place at last, he stops and looks out over the shimmering level Ohio. A large old-fashioned stern-wheeler is passing, churning up the water and casting a long wake. He knows Ann Lee is riding the stern-wheeler but he cannot see her and he knows it is useless to shout. The boat is passing. She is passing, going on down the Ohio to the Mississippi.

He wakes up, chilled and trembling, begins to slap his hands together and stamp his feet, rousing his circulation, careless of stares.

They are coming into the suburbs of Louisville, riding now along a smaller highway which parallels the railroad track and the valley, with big frame houses hidden behind the trees. Colby looks out of the window, waiting for it to end, trying to remember that pain does not last any longer than happiness and leaves no more permanent marks.

Then they are gliding smoothly past the stockyards, under the last bridge. The neighborhood which was once rowdy with farmers' bars is now transformed, painted, inhabited by the young; there are baby carriages on the cracked old sidewalks. Colby tries to imagine living in one of the while shot-gun houses with Ann Lee, tries to imagine her with furni-ture, pots and pans, a closet full of clothes.

They weave along, in and out of the slow traffic. Colby looks down on the roofs of cars, sees them glint in the sun.

The bus draws up, groaning, at the station, and the door wheezes open. Colby is out first.

Cool air brushes his face and he sees I. and Martha stand-ing hooked up in a patch of sunlight next to the station. They are looking away from him at something which has caught their attention on the other side of the parking lot. Martha is carrying the baby in a canvas sling suspended from one shoulder.

Colby stops dead. He stares at them. They do not feel the weight of his look. After a minute, Martha glances around and sees him, then starts forward with a look of concern.

I. follows behind her with small steps. Colby can see his long face over Martha's shoulder.

I. says, "We called the theater, they don't know anything."

Martha is pressing Colby's shoulder, kneading it as though to remove a pain."

"They don't know where she is," I. says.

"Oh, Colby," Martha says.

He turns away from them and hangs his head. The tears which have been pent up for the last eight hours move closer to the edges of his eyes, then surge and sweep over, running down his face, burning hot.

Martha says, "Don't cry," and I. remonstrates with her.

Colby turns to look at them. He sees that the baby is wak-ing up, stirring in the sack, one hand waving.

Colby says, "She told me she was going to go down the river. She told me that at the beginning."

They both look at him, waiting.

"I can't lose her," Colby says.

The baby is beginning to drone.

"I have a feeling it's already happened," Martha says.

"No. It hasn't happened yet. We can find her. We can take your car and find her."

"Colby . . . I don't know . . . The thing is . . ."

"We have to take your car and find her. I can't do it alone."

The baby is rocking into full-scale crying now, her face wrinkled up.

"Will you take me?" Colby asks.

The faces of his old friends hover. He sees them glare and grimace, pass silent messages back and forth, Martha shifting from foot to foot to quiet the baby.

"Where's the car?" Colby asks. "We have to get started."

"Where to?" I.'s voice is soft.

"Down the Ohio to Cairo. Down the Mississippi to New Orleans . . ."

I. turns, takes one step, his ragged sneaker placed firmly. "Here we go!" he says, reaching for Colby's arm.

But Martha is there. She is there so quickly that later Colby can't remember when she moved to I.'s side. She holds out the baby — towards I., towards Colby.

Colby is about to begin to explain how everything can be arranged when he feels I.'s hand drop from his arm.

Colby turns around. Across the parking lot, another bus has pulled up; it waits, its motor idling.

He runs towards it.

Behind him, he hears sounds — protests, he imagines, exclamations, even reproaches. None of it matters. He is seeing the brown Ohio curling into the darker Mississippi; he is seeing the bright blue eye of the Gulf.

As he approaches, the bus door wheezes open.